CHAPTER ONE

Karen

What are you afraid of? The damning question hangs ever present in my mind as I try to concentrate on my work. I've read the email in front of me over a dozen times without taking in a single word. It's gotten to the point where each letter I attempt to digest is looking like it's come from a foreign language. What are you afraid of? How can I answer such a delicate topic in only a few breaths?

The question came from my roommate, Beth, during a random yet innocent conversation. The words rolled off her tongue like sweat from a forehead mere moments before she left for a week. How long had she been waiting to ask me? Days? Weeks? Months? From the first moment we met? It doesn't matter. She asked me. I didn't answer of course, but now she knows there's a glimpse of something deep down within my core I cannot express, something that keeps me trapped inside this house day and night, forcing me to work three separate jobs from the safety of my study as a virtual assistant.

Barred windows cast a thick shadow over the room through thinning curtains, interspersed with the light from a full moon. I only allow the glow from my laptop's monitor to balance out the contrast as I stare like a zombie at an instant messaging window on my computer, waiting for my next task.

I live just outside of downtown Phoenix, Arizona in a two-bedroom one-bathroom house I can only just afford to rent. My home is too close to the city, driving up the cost of housing in the area, so much so it forces me to take in a college student from time to time to keep my strict budget intact. Fortunately, I have a locked-in fixed rental agreement that won't be changing anytime soon. At least I hope it won't.

I sometimes wonder if it even matters where I live. I don't leave this house unless I have no other choice. Most of my time is spent plugged in online, set between paid employment and pointless activities. Both eat up the hours until I fall asleep and forget about it all. It's not exactly the life I imagined having at thirty-five.

Most of the VA work I do is at night. It's the only way to communicate effectively with my contacts in the UK during their business hours. My days currently start at midnight depending on how the two time zones shift back and forth throughout the year. I organize meetings, sift through and respond to urgent emails, and cut down the time barrier that exists between two executives who live on either side of the globe. It's boring on a good day like any job, but when there's enough work, it pays the bills and keeps me busy.

The cursor on my laptop blinks on a loop. I stare at the animation as if it could change at any moment, knowing it never will. I feel like I'm stuck between worlds as I wait.

What are you afraid of? I know Beth meant nothing by it, but it's a question that most of the people I take in will never ask me no matter how much they might want to. It's so obvious to the casual observer that something is keeping me cooped up in here like a rat in a cage. No, not something, but someone.

I shake the thought, not needing the distraction. I am about to sit in on a meeting via video chat and take down crucial notes for one of my bosses so he can have everything he needs first thing when he wakes up six hours from now. The Internet has spoiled these people. Of course, these meetings don't always happen in any predictable pattern. And to top it all off, I'm not allowed to record these sessions due to a strict privacy policy the UK company enforces.

When it comes down to it, I am paid to make someone else's perfect life better while mine continues to be a struggle.

What are you afraid of? The question echoes in my mind.

Before my work starts, I minimize the window to my desktop and stare at the one background image that keeps me going through these late-night hours. I've seen it a thousand times, but it never fails to take me aside from the anxiety these meetings generate.

Champagne Beach, Vanuatu stares back at me with its perfect blue water and near white sands. Every week I get paid, I put as much of my modest income aside as I can to save up for a long-awaited holiday to the South Pacific island. I'd move there if I could, far away from the world, far away from its people, but I doubt that I would ever be so lucky.

Saving up enough money for this trip is only a matter of time. The real dispute is whether I'll be able to find the courage to walk out the front door of this house and go on the vacation.

CHAPTER TWO

With a sigh, I switch to my IM app again and meeting. Thoughts of my life make me circle back to my roommate Beth. Why did she have to ask me that question? We had a good thing going between us. She didn't pry too deep into my story and I didn't prompt her to. It was the perfect superficial level of communication we shared given our relationship's short three-month lifespan. We were starting to get along there for a minute. What had changed? I won't know until she returns from her week-long trip.

My contact, Julia Thomas, comes online and types out her standard greeting.

Julia Thomas: Hello, Karen. How are you?
Karen Rainey: I'm fine.

I reply with the least amount of words possible. I've never met Julia before in the real world and never will. For that reason and others combined, there's no need for anything to form between us beyond what is necessary to get through the meeting.

After we go through the boilerplate VA security checks and agreements, I am told that the session will start in five minutes. I have little idea what this is about, but I understand that it's important from the multiple emails my boss David sent. My head is elsewhere though.

I take a deep breath in and let it back out as I locate my oversize coffee mug. The double strength brew is the only thing that will get me through this gathering of suits. I stifle a yawn and realize I'll never get used to these hours no matter how long I work them. It's hard not to fall asleep during one of these boring meetings, especially when you aren't actually present in a room full of stuffy career-focused men and women. I would never want to be like them if I'm being honest.

The low guttural sound of a car rolls by the outside of my house, drawing away my attention as the bass of a heavy beat drones on in the background. My street isn't the busiest during the day, so any time a vehicle comes past in the middle of the night, I feel my skin crawl for a slight moment. I grab my smartphone and bring up a security camera app. I have surveillance equipment and sensors fitted all around the entire property. It cost me a lot of money to install—more than I could afford when I had them installed—but it's worth every penny to have that sense of control.

What are you afraid of?

The question makes me fumble with my phone. I take a moment to focus on my cell to see the car as it finishes rolling by the camera at the left side of the home. A carload of people in their twenties fills the seats. They're all drinking from what I can tell and are most likely heading downtown. They look like college kids out for fun and nothing more.

I pray they don't stop.

By the time the car continues past my residence without stopping, the meeting has gotten underway. I realize that one executive on screen is speaking toward me.

"David's VA. Are you there?"

There's no point for him to learn my name, so I don't let his rudeness bother me. I press the button on my wireless headset that activates its built-in microphone. "Uh, yes. I'm here," I say to a large room with real people in it. Who knows how many digital eyes are spying in on this session?

"Good. Does David have any questions before we get underway? I know he's shown concern regarding a few key areas. I want to make sure we don't miss a thing."

As my eyes bulge in my head, I switch my screen to a new tab and open the email from my boss. I didn't see any queries he wanted asked, but then again, I tend to skim his emails.

"Well?" the impatient man reiterates.

"Just a second, sorry," I say. My emails are taking longer than normal to load on my aging laptop. The cheap hunk of plastic is close to being tossed out onto the scrap heap and I can't afford a replacement at the moment.

Finally, I locate the email and see that David mentioned something about questions and even had an attachment to boot. How did I miss this? I scurry to download what the jerk needs and move back to the meeting.

"Found them, sorry."

"It's about bloody time," the man says, glaring at me in low resolution with his British accent from over five thousand miles away. "David will hear about this if you don't hurry."

I blurt out the first question of three, hoping to silence the jerk. He quiets down and bites his lip. I can tell I'm just one tiny mistake away from him reporting my incompetence to my boss, and all over a few lousy seconds of time I've cost him. It would be enough to get me fired too. I've screwed up so much lately. My mind is all over the place, and David gives me the most work out of the people I VA for. Losing him would be devastating.

I finish the questions and feel some sense of relief as the focus of the room pulls away from me. Even though I'm not physically there and can't be seen on video chat, I still shake my head with embarrassment.

My contact for the meeting chimes in with a question for me over the chat window.

Is everything okay?

I type back a lie and say how grateful I am for the concern. It's the first time she has said anything besides work-related nonsense I care little about. It almost brings a smile to my face. I'm far from okay, and I don't see my situation changing anytime soon.

The meeting reaches its halfway point without stopping as I finish my coffee. I'm tempted to run off and make another, but I might miss something vital, not that I understand what it is we are talking about. Once, I tried to spend a few hours getting to know what it is my boss does for a living, but boredom set in the way it always does.

My tenth yawn for the night falls out of me when the British jerk calls out again. I don't hear every word he rattles off and soon find all eyes pointed to the camera I get my feed from.

"Well?" the impatient man says yet again.

When I go to answer, a notification pops up on my phone along with a sound. I grab it, unable to resist the distraction, and look down at the screen to see the one message that only sends a chill down my spine:

There is motion at your front door.

CHAPTER THREE

I have to read the notification on my phone twice before it sinks in. I tap the alert and wait as the screen prepares to stream the front door camera to me. The spinning circle takes too long for my liking until it finally finishes loading. There, on my cell, stands a man just outside the front of my house, bathed in shadow, his hood all the way up over his head. I freeze and continue to stare.

What do I do? Do I call the police? Do I scream and hope one of my neighbors hears me? They wouldn't try to save me though. I've made it my mission not to get to know them. They see me as the crazed shut-in of the street. I think of Beth but remember that she won't be back for another few days.

I rise from my chair in a hurry, smartphone still out displaying the very stiff man who is staring at my front door. I dash along and beyond my tiny study, through to my combined kitchen, living and dining area. Mess stains the flooring and walls as I rush on through to a hallway that leads to my bedroom. I unlock the door to my room with a set of keys from my pocket and charge for a baseball bat I have hidden by my bed. I'd keep a gun in the house instead, but I can't stand the things.

What are you afraid of? The question hits me at the worst of times and makes me trip over. I collect the baseball bat and jump to my feet.

I stare at the guy in my phone as he remains in the same position as before. As I struggle to find the courage to stand tall, the man turns away and slowly wanders off, leaving a box in his place. I quickly try the next camera with a shaky finger and see him continuing on toward the left side of my house along the footpath without a second thought.

"What the hell?" I say out loud through a choked breath.

I don't know what to make of what's just happened as a noise in my wireless headset continues to complain. It's the jerk from the meeting questioning my professionalism while he simultaneously moans about virtual assistants.

I plant the baseball bat back in its place and rush for my study. But before I reach the entrance to my small office, curiosity holds me for a moment, eventually driving me to the front door instead. I can hear the executive complaining bitterly to his coworkers, so I press a button on my headset and relay a quick message that I will return in a minute. It should give me a chance to think of an excuse.

I don't know why I feel the overwhelming desire to learn what's inside the box or why it has been left for me at one in the morning, but I figure the damage is done with the meeting. I can quickly grab the package and take it with me to the angry executive. Whatever lie I tell him I'll also say to my boss when I report in later.

I reach my front door and push my headset down to my neck so I no longer hear anyone else's voice competing with my thoughts. I need to concentrate if I'm going to be opening the front door, especially at this hour.

What was the strange man doing here so late? Was he a delivery guy who'd forgotten a package in his run and thought he'd get it delivered before he started his next shift? I wasn't expecting anything, but I do order a lot online. Packages come early and late, but never like this.

I unlock three of four active deadbolts that litter my front door. I stopped using the fourth lock after a while as it meant getting inside upon my return was taking too long. I edge the door open an inch at a time while I cycle through each camera on my smartphone. All is clear in both directions. The road is empty. I take in a deep breath and rush outside through the small gap I've created in the door. I scoop up the box and realize it's quite a bit lighter than I expected.

I move inside and lock all four deadbolts on the front door as if the apocalypse is coming despite the street being clear. With my package under my arm, I head back to my meeting and apologize to everyone in the room, claiming that I had an emergency I had to deal with. No one bothers to ask what that situation was or if I'm okay except my contact via the chat window. I type a reply to her as quickly as possible thanking her for the concern.

The jerk speaks again. "If we could get back to business, that would be great. I'm sure David would appreciate it if we actually got something done today."

I ignore the comment from the head suit who has been running the session and quickly open the package before he gets underway with his next line of boredom. I might as well. I've ruined the meeting as it is.

There doesn't seem to be any shipping labels or stickers on the box to tell me who sent the damn thing. I know I shouldn't be opening it. There could be anything inside like drugs or money. This could have been left at the wrong place and be meant for someone else. Too late though. I've broken through the packing tape.

I carefully fold open the lids and see a lot of screwed up brown paper filling the contents to protect something small. There in the middle is a thick piece of white cardboard. I lift it up delicately with my fingertips and unfold what appears to be a note. My eyes land on the words and read them whether I want to or not.

I drop the note and the box and fly up out of my seat. I realize in an instant why I'm receiving a strange package in the middle of the night. The box falls fast and tumbles about the ground, but I can't escape the card as it lands face up. I see the messages again written in Latin cursive, centered for my eyes only.

Omnia mors aequat.

Like a drone, I stammer the rough translation out loud. "Death makes all equal."

CHAPTER FOUR

This can't be happening. This can't be real. I didn't just receive a package with next to nothing in it, but a threatening note written in Latin. But it stares back at me, defying my every thought. Once I wrap my head around the concept, I come to terms with the simple fact that the piece of card could have only been sent by one man: my ex.

The UK meeting continues on screen in the background without me taking down a single letter as my headset dangles from my neck. I drop out of the gathering, not giving an excuse. There's no way in hell I'll be able to concentrate and take down the key points now. I've got bigger problems than losing my job to worry about.

I leave the box in my study and rush out of the room to make sure every lock on the front door is secured along with the side entry. They are the only ways into this small house. After I triple check each door, I walk around and feel how strong each bar is on all the windows. If my ex wants to break into my home, he's got his work cut out for him. But then again, I know him. If he craves something, he'll find a way. He always has. I can't stop this.

My feet rush me back to the study so I can pace up and down the room.

I eventually sit on my office chair and feel my eyes twitch as I try to accept what is happening. Has he found me? Was that him before? Or is this just a big joke? It has to be, right? He can't be out of lockup.

Why now though? Why after five years of being careful? I thought with the pathetic life I live, practically locked away in my prison I call a home, that I could one day put him to the back of my mind and never have to worry about the truth. I grab a look at the background on my computer of that perfect beach in Vanuatu and allow fear to seize me. Will I ever see that unadulterated water? Will my bare feet ever feel the powdery sand between my toes? He'll reach me before I get my chance. I know it.

My cell beeps with an email notification. It's Julia from the UK meeting. No doubt she wants to learn what happened. She only cares because my boss David won't receive his critical notes from her company. Whatever deal they were about to broker will be delayed all because of my inability to deliver. Well screw it. I don't care anymore. There are more significant things in this world than some virtual job. I can always dip into my holiday money to survive. I can run further into hiding.

With my phone in hand, I remember the cameras I have rigged up to the house. They are motion activated, but I only get a notification when someone reaches the front door. Otherwise, I'd be bugged every time a person or a car moved by in the street.

With that in mind, I search back to the event at the front door and watch from two different angles as the man casually walks up to my house with the box in his hand and a hood over his head. He keeps his face down low and out of sight within his sweatshirt the whole time. It's as if he has done this before. Or worse still, he knew where the cameras would be.

I scrunch up my brow as I watch the footage over and over. Why couldn't I have sprung for the better model, one with a much clearer image? This isn't the moment to curse myself though. I have to keep a level head and think of my next move. God knows my ex is probably anticipating my every thought. But he can't know everything. There's no way he can know about the go bag I have stashed away filled with clothing, money, a fake passport, and a can of pepper spray, does he? On the off chance this day should ever come about, I prepared that backpack and stuffed it deep in my closet. But things haven't reached that point yet, have they? I need to hold up for a moment to breathe and—

My cell beeps again, alerting me that someone is at the front door. He's back.

CHAPTER FIVE

I unlock my phone in a hurry and open the notification with slippery fingers. The few seconds of loading take far too long in my brain to comprehend as my lungs struggle to function. If only I could afford a newer smartphone. Finally, the camera mounted in the front's corner door activates to show me a familiar face. It's Beth, back early. I practically fall into a heap with relief when I view her unlocking the door.

I close the app and come out of the study, needing to meet Beth in the flesh to stop myself from going crazy. She unlocks a few deadbolts and tries to push through the door not realizing I had set the fourth one neither of us ever used. It's practically industrial and hard to work with.

"Why won't this open?" Beth's muffled voice asks on the other side of the door. I'll need to think up an excuse as to why I set the fourth bolt.

Heading over to the front door, I use my key to help Beth get inside. She stumbles through when I undo the final obstacle in her way. I see the travel bags in her hands. She's only twenty-three and has been away visiting her folks during a break from school. Like my previous housemates, Beth's a college student studying at the downtown campus. This, in fact, is an early return for her, by a few days.

"Whoa, hey Karen. I hope I didn't disturb you while you were working or whatever," she says fresh faced as if it isn't one in the morning. She's a slim pretty young woman who I'd kill to look like. She brushes her perfect blonde hair out of her face, waiting for an answer.

"No, it's fine, Beth," I say glancing toward my study entrance. "I've finished up for the night." *And possibly for every other night after*, I think. I'm not looking forward to dealing with David in the morning.

"What's the deal with the front door? We never set that big lock. Is something up?"

Beth follows her quick interrogation with a light slap on the door. I need to change the subject fast. I don't want her to get involved in all of this. She doesn't deserve to be caught up in my problems.

"Why are you home a few days early? And this late?" I ask.

She scrunches her nose at me, possibly confused by my poorly phrased question.

I do what I can to cover. "I mean, I thought you'd be home in a couple of days at a reasonable hour."

"Oh, right. I had a fight with my parents and took the last bus here. Best I don't get into it."

"Fair enough," I say. "Can I make you a coffee or something?" I ask as I check if the front door is properly secured including the big lock. I use the firm grip I need on the bolt as a means to calm my shaking self down. It helps a little.

"Sure, why not? I'm too wired to sleep yet anyway. I'm still in travel mode." She falls into the small sofa we have in the combined living and dining section of the house. The kitchen is partially walled off to the side of the area. "I'm not keeping you up, am I?"

"No. Unfortunately, I was working. Luckily, I'm finished now though," I say with a half-smile. I think about when I'd come home this late at Beth's age. It wouldn't be from taking a bus back home from my parents. It'd be from some crazy party I attended. I got up to some wild things. Beth would be shocked to hear even half of it. But I'm not proud of those days. They led me to him, which in turn set about the worst night of my life. One I'll never forget no matter how much I try.

"Wait, you didn't tell me about the front door," Beth says again.

I close my eyes for a moment and hunch. She won't let it go. I have to give her something. Turning back to her with a reassuring smile, I say the first thing that occurs. "I thought I heard a noise is all. Just being careful."

"Oh, okay," Beth says being used to my overzealous methods when it comes to security. She might not have access to the cameras, but she knows they are there and thinks they are a waste of time. She doesn't recognize the reason I need them though. If only I could tell someone about it. But I appreciate that would be a huge mistake, one I promised to never make.

"What noise did you hear?"

Damn her ability to detect a problem. I try not to react to her question, but my body language says it all as I start to pace on the spot.

Beth's brows narrow in.

"I don't know. It was probably nothing. I'm just being careful is all. You never know what could happen, so I try to stay safe."

"Safe? More like you're trapped in this place. You need to chill out and forget all this high-tech security crap. You remind me of my parents. They're always scared of the world because they watch too much news. Just live a little, you know?"

I smile and nod politely. It's this kind of conversation that makes her ask me what I'm so afraid of. "You're probably right," I say. It's best to agree and move on so she forgets the whole thing. I can't have her digging around and asking me questions I never want to answer. I've made it this far. I had until that note appeared. Now I don't know what to think or what will happen next.

I feel my stomach fill with rocks. Beth's company is helping me forget for a moment about my problems. She's good like this. If only chatting away to her could cause them to all disappear into thin air.

I walk Beth's black coffee over to her and set it down on our stained table. The house came furnished with enough existing flaws to make it impossible to tell the difference between a new mark and an old one.

"Thanks," she says, picking up her coffee straight away. She slurps it down as if it's not scalding her throat. I shake my head at her, the way I always do, and sip and blow on my white coffee with sugar.

We sit in silence, enjoying our drinks for a moment. I stare at Beth and feel happy she is home early. Most people in my situation don't want to accept in a housemate, but I didn't do so without doing my research first. A background check revealed nothing out of the ordinary. Plus, her age works well in her favor. There's no possible way she could be linked to my past.

I welcome whatever comfort I can from the warm drink in my hands as it draws me gently from reality for a split second. The swirling combination closes my eyes and consumes my senses for a moment before the gravity of the world pulls me back down again.

"No, wait," Beth blurts out as she sits up straight. "I know what's got you on edge; it's an ex-boyfriend."

I spill part of my coffee onto my hands and stare at her trying to understand why she just said those words.

She returns my gaze with a crooked smile and says, "I'm right, aren't I."

My mouth falls open and responds whether I want it to or not. "How did you know?"

CHAPTER SIX

I continue to stare at Beth as she analyses my reaction. I respond with confusion, begging to understand why she so suddenly asked me if I was on edge because of an ex-boyfriend. How, through her fatigued mind, did she conjure up that result?

I repeat my last question to her, somehow hoping it might change things. "Seriously, how did you know?"

"Come on," Beth says, "What else could it be?"

"Anything. I heard a noise. I wanted to be extra cautious. Hell, because I felt like it. What made you jump to that conclusion?"

Beth drinks the rest of her coffee as if it's not still burning hot. She wipes her mouth and rises to her feet before taking a few steps toward me. I feel my heart pound harder. Does she know the truth about me? Does she know about my ex? I unconsciously step back from her until I crash into the refrigerator.

"Whoa," she says, "are you okay?"

I nod. "Sorry, just a bit jumpy is all."

Beth continues to walk by me into the kitchen to the sink. She speaks over her shoulder while she runs the tap. "Anyway, to answer your question, it's always an ex, in my experience at least. Sometimes they can't stand the thought of you moving on with another person, so they try to make your life a living hell until you either take them back or move away. Are you seeing someone?"

I scoff. "Definitely not."

"Okay, well, maybe your ex thinks you are and has lost it a little."

I shake my head. Why does she know so much about the topic? "Is this something that's happened to you?" I ask.

Beth pauses. "Not me directly, but to my last housemate—a friend really—when I lived closer to the campus. This guy just became obsessed with her. He followed her to her class. Went to every party she attended. When she said she wasn't interested, he lost it, and things took a sharp turn. Soon he was showing up at our apartment in the middle of the night drunk out of his mind, demanding she be with him. We had to call the cops like six times, but he still didn't get the message. So, eventually we both moved out and thought it best to go our own ways, you know?"

I shook my head, thinking about Beth's friend. I knew the pain she'd experienced. But my problem is more than some college crush though and is complex to say the least.

"So, do you have ex trouble like my friend did?" Beth asks.

I focus my eyes on her with an open mouth. "It's complicated."

"Oh, come on," Beth says as she goes to leave the kitchen. "Don't give me that line. I won't tell anyone."

I hold her gently with both arms on her shoulders. "You don't understand."

"If you aren't interested in talking about it, that's fine," she says, breaking free of my grip without any force.

My mouth opens to speak, but I stop myself short. She is right. I can't lie to her face and say everything will be okay, because the truth is simple: I have no idea what will happen next.

"But, seeing as you've been cool to live with for the last three months, I'll let you have your little secret, for now." She gives me a cheeky grin.

I stare at her for too long until she speaks again.

"Bring it in." She opens up for a hug. I'm not much of a hugger but I take the gesture and wrap my arms around her. All I can hope in this moment as she squeezes me too tightly is that she forgets everything we've talked about for the last few minutes in the morning and doesn't mention it again.

Time will tell.

CHAPTER SEVEN

I head to my room after grabbing my laptop from my study. I bring along a strong cup of coffee to keep me going as sleep is the last thing on my mind. Although a solid eight-hour nap would do me some good, I need to focus on my next move if this note has any meaning behind it.

I still can't believe the message I received. If it means what I think it does, then I could be in great danger. My thoughts quickly shift to Beth. Is she at risk just by living in the same house as me? Should I grab my things and go now to keep her safe? No. I know my ex wouldn't harm an innocent woman despite it all. I'm the one he wants, right?

Plonking down on my bed, I realize I need to take action fast before I breakdown into a useless wreck if I'm going to get ahead of this thing. I pull out my cell again and review the footage of the man delivering the box. There's something about him that is still niggling at the corners of my mind. I know if I examine the recording enough times, I'll find what I need to point me in the right direction.

I watch the event from all three cameras I have installed at the front of the house. The footage confirms it's not my ex I'm seeing delivering the package. The height and shape of the man's figure doesn't match. My ex is far taller and thinner than the man who I see standing at my front door like a zombie. Plus, my ex couldn't physically be here seeing as he is locked up behind bars in one of the most secure facilities in the country.

He's not supposed to know where I am, especially considering the distance I moved away from where I used to live. I guess he finally found me and thought he would have some thug deliver a note to remind me of the past. Did that mean he would then send this person back to take things to the next level?

The two wide-angled cameras before the front door fail to reveal much other than a determined individual who doesn't appear to be phased by my surveillance system. His hood hides his face perfectly from every position. Then it hits me.

How did he know I had the setup? I've gone to great lengths to hide the cameras away underneath the guttering of the house, so they don't stick out. Most people want you to see the security cameras they've had installed. I don't. I prefer individuals to act the way they normally would as if they thought they weren't being recorded.

The front camera captures the creepiest part of the man's delivery. It's where he takes his time approaching the door. He seems all too aware of the single step up to the boxed-in portico entrance. Again, I know this isn't the man who actually sent the card, but someone who he paid to make the drop off. I have to continue reminding myself that to prevent my heart from exploding.

Has this delivery man been here before? Was he given a detailed layout of the exterior of my house? I continue to watch as he stands still after placing the package on the ground. What is his deal?

Wait! I back up the footage to the moment he bends over to place the box down. The black-and-white image before me isn't very clear, but there's enough there for me to identify a familiar tattoo that's wrapped around the forearm of a pizza delivery guy I know named Emilio.

Every time I order in a pizza, he's the one to drop if off without fail. I always give him a little extra for the tip as he is never late. Not only is he my pizza guy, but he lives down the street from me with his grandma.

I get my confirmation when he raises his head up enough for the camera to catch a glimpse of his soup-strainer mustache. I'd recognize it anywhere. It has to be him.

"What the hell are you doing?" I ask out loud. I cycle through the footage again and stare at Emilio as he bends down to reveal his tattoo on his forearm of Sister Mary with her palms together. Sure, it's a common symbol, but how many guys get this particular thing tattooed on their forearm instead of their bicep?

Equipped with more than I thought I'd find, I decide it's time to order in a pizza, but I have to wait until morning given the hour. I look up the company's number on my cell having used them so many times in the past. I read their trading hours and realize they don't open until eleven. The discovery sends a sigh out of my mouth as I push my rear up to the wall my bed is pressed against. I stare at my bedroom door, knowing it's going to be a long night.

CHAPTER EIGHT

I didn't sleep a wink. Instead, I sat with my back firm against the wall, baseball bat in hand while my cell automatically cycled through each security camera while on charge. When morning came, inching its way into existence via the twittering of birds and the dampening of distant sounds, I checked, once every hour, to see if Beth had emerged from her room but she must have been sleeping in.

Eleven ticks over on my cell. With bleary eyes, I dial out to my pizza place and wait almost ten rings before I get an answer.

"Louie's Pizza," says a busy man on the other end over the sound of chatty staff and industrial ovens.

"Hi, I'd like to order a large pepperoni pizza for delivery please."

"One large pepperoni," he says slowly, no doubt writing the order out. "Anything else?"

"Yeah, I'll need it to be delivered by Emilio."

The man on the phone pauses. "Come again?"

"I want my pizza delivered by Emilio."

"Is this a damn joke? I don't have time for pranks. We're prepping for the lunch rush."

"It's no joke. I'll pay double if you don't believe me. Can you send him? Is he on today?"

The man mutters away, probably thinking I can't hear him cursing in the shop. I'm sure he's heard it all before working in the industry. "Fine, but you'll have to wait until he gets in. Also, I want payment upfront. Whatever this is, I get paid first."

"Deal. I'll get my credit card," I say, not revealing a single thing about my odd request.

***

An hour ticks by when I hear a quick knock at the front door just after receiving a notification on my cell. The connection reveals Emilio standing nervously in the portico. I can't believe he actually came. The thought makes me doubt my suspicions somewhat. Could he really be so stupid to show up here the next day after leaving a threatening message on someone else's behalf? Then another harsh idea comes at me in a hurry. What if someone has paid him to come here and attack me? What the hell was I thinking ordering a pizza and requesting to have him deliver it?

Before panic sets in, I unlock the four deadbolts and open the front door a crack to see his nervous face greet me. "Hello," I say with a whisper.

"Pizza delivery from Louie's. It's all paid up."

Emilio's in a hurry, wanting to get this over with as quickly as possible. Sweat slides down his forehead despite it not being a warm day for Arizona.

I run my eyes up and down his body before opening the door any further. I spot the tattoo again on his forearm, confirming he was the one who delivered that box last night. I continue to stare and attempt to determine if he's got a weapon hidden away ready to pull out the second I come out to grab the pizza. My scan fails to help, given the baggy clothes the guy is wearing.

I push the door halfway open and reach out to take the pizza box as he slides it out from a delivery bag. I grip it in two hands and bring the package in, placing it down in a rush on the kitchen bench.

Emilio goes to leave. "Wait," I call out, realizing he will not attack. "Don't you want your tip?"

"Oh, yeah," he says with a smile. His shoulders relax. He thinks he's off the hook. I reach into my purse and drag out a fifty-dollar bill. His eyes light up, expecting me to hand it over. I inch the note toward him but tear it back at the last second. I then bring out an object from behind the door Emilio is all too aware of.

A wave of nerves pours from his face.

I clear my throat and gather as much courage as I can. "This fifty is yours," I say, "if you tell me why you delivered this box to me at one this morning."

Emilio shifts his eyes to mine. I can't work out if he is about to run away or attack me.

We stare at each other in silence.

CHAPTER NINE

Emilio contemplates running. I can see it in his eyes as they shift left and right, trying to find an escape from the situation he's allowed himself to fall into. I have to act fast. "Please," I say, finding my voice. "Don't run. I just want some answers. Nothing else. I promise you're not in any kind of trouble."

He takes a step backward as if I'm a police officer struggling to talk him down from a ledge. "No, screw you. I'm out of here." He turns to leave.

"Wait. I'll give you another fifty. That's a hundred-dollar tip for a few quick questions."

He pauses with his back to me, frozen with indecision. I don't know whether to be happy or annoyed. I couldn't afford to offer him the initial fifty dollars let alone a full hundred. If he needs more than this to stay, I'm screwed.

Emilio turns around. "You got two minutes. Then I'm out."

"That's all I need," I say. I hold up the second note next to the first. He snatches the money and strolls toward me. I step aside, holding the door open for him to enter. He walks into my house, muttering away to himself. Beth is still in her room. If she sees Emilio, it will only generate more questions from her sharp mind I don't have the energy to answer.

"Alright. Your two minutes is ticking down." He crosses his arms.

I try to think of what to say to him. I thought I knew what I wanted to ask but staring at this heavyset man only makes me want to beg him to reveal all he knows. I have to keep it together.

"Time's wasting," he says.

"I know," I say as I grab the box with the Latin note in it. Clearing my throat, I focus on Emilio as best I can. "I need to know who asked you to drop off this package. That's all."

He shrugs. "I don't know what to tell you. I was mid-shift at my job last night, and some dude comes up and offers me two hundred bucks to deliver this box to some place without ringing the bell or knocking on the door."

"That's it? Just drop it off and leave?"

"No, he told me to wear a hoodie to cover my face and to wait until the middle of the night. He warned me about the cameras. I realized when I got the address it was your house I'd be making the drop to. I didn't even know you had cameras. I almost changed my mind, but it was too late by then."

I shake my head, wanting to scold him for doing this to one of his regular customers and a neighbor, but I bite my tongue. "So, this man, what did he look like?"

Emilio shrugs. "Just some dude in a suit. Late forties, long brown hair, five o'clock shadow, strong build, and tall. He drove a black SUV. I don't know what else to say."

These qualities in no means describe the man I fear. Emilio sounds like he was given money by a criminal hiding in a suit or some lawyer. None of my ex's associates dress in that manner.

"Is that it? Can I go?" Emilio asks.

"Wait. This man, did he say anything else? Did he tell you why he wanted you to do this?"

Emilio stared away in thought for a moment. "No. Just deliver the box for two hundred bucks. That, with your offer, has made my week a decent one for a change."

I snap. Before I can stop myself, I'm grabbing Emilio by his shirt collar. "This is my life we're talking about here. Do you think I care about you making a quick buck? Now please, tell me what else he said to you. There has to be something."

Emilio holds up both his palms, not wanting to push me off. He lets my feeble attempt to subdue him work. "That's all I know. I swear."

I try to shove him toward the front door. He moves. "You don't understand. He's coming for me. It's only a matter of time."

"Screw this." Emilio grabs the handle of the unlocked entry with both hands and jiggles it open in a hurry. He rushes straight through the opening as soon as he can. My phone buzzes in my pocket the second he sets off the motion sensor in the portico. I'll have great footage of him running off. I can only imagine he'll tell the owner of the pizza shop I'm crazy and to put me on a list of banned customers. Fine by me. I'll never order from there again.

I fight back an ocean of tears that want to spew out of my eyes as I close the door and engage each lock, one at a time. How can this day get any worse?

"What was all that about?" Beth asks me.

Oh crap. I spin round, looking guilty as hell and give her a forced smile that almost hurts my face. She's standing in the entry to the hallway wearing a T-shirt and shorts. How much has she heard?

"Karen? What's happening? Who was that guy?"

My fake grin fades in a heartbeat as I shake my head. "I don't know what to say."

"This is about your ex, isn't it?"

I nod.

"I think it's time you told me what's going on."

I walk toward my bedroom, trying to go by her.

Beth moves out and stands in my way. "Are you serious? You can't expect me to listen to all that and just forget it."

"Please," I say, staring into her eyes. "For your own sake, pretend you didn't hear a word."

Beth scoffs. "You begged that delivery guy for information on your ex. What's so dangerous about this man of yours? Should I call the cops?"

My head drops. I can't ignore the problem any longer. I have to either tell Beth the truth or advise her to find somewhere else to live. She deserves none of the trouble that could come my way.

Beth steps closer and places both hands on my shoulders. I fall to pieces and throw myself into her. She wraps her arms around me and holds on tight while I fail to hold back my tears.

"You don't understand," I blubber. "I'm not allowed to tell you. I'm not supposed to say anything about him."

"About who?" Beth asks, keeping her voice down.

"About my ex."

We pull apart from each other. Beth's brows have twisted in toward the bridge of her nose. "Why can't you talk about him? Does he have that much of a hold over you?"

"No, it's not that. He's..." I trail off, knowing I've already revealed more than I should. Why can't I keep it together?

"Karen? What is it? You realize you can tell me anything."

My eyes lift from the floor to her confused face. I barely know her, but she's the only person in my life right now. I have no one else. No one. I can't hold this in any longer. It's been five years of secrets, lies, and non-stop anxiety. It's coming out whether or not I want it to.

"My ex. His name is... his name's not important, but he is in prison serving a life sentence."

"Holy crap," Beth blurts out. "Sorry, I didn't mean to say that. It was just unexpected."

"That's not all," I say, putting her back on track.

"There's more?"

I nod, closing my eyes for a moment. "The only reason he's serving such a long sentence is because of me. I testified against him in court about a crime I witnessed him commit. That got him locked up for good. I went into hiding under witness protection straight away with the help of the Department of Justice. But now, after five years, I'm certain Zach has found me. I think he might be sending someone to this house to harm me."

CHAPTER TEN

I watch as Beth paces up and down a small space in the living area with one hand on her head and the other planted on her hip. Her eyes dart back and forth as they try to understand what exactly I had just said to her.

"This is bad, Karen," Beth says. "This is extremely bad. I mean, I can handle most things. Not much gets me rattled, but if this is true, it's crazy."

"I know it is, believe me. Not a day goes by that I don't think about it. That constant reminder forces me to live the way I do. I've lived the last five years of my life as a nobody, hiding away from society, avoiding people, while only rarely leaving this place. I order everything online. I work from the study in there as a VA because it's the only job I can get from the house with my skill set. Unless it can be done on the web, I don't dare step a foot out of this building out of a fear that Zach or one of his friends might find me."

Beth's mouth has fallen open during my rant. So much so she places herself down on the sofa as if to take it all in. I've blown her mind with my messed-up world. She probably thought I was just some boring shut-in who'd done nothing crazy in her miserable life. Beth does not know about my past or the stupid things I've done being the girlfriend of a notorious criminal. But that time of my life came crashing down hard. So much so, I can't stand to think about it.

"I have so many questions," Beth says. "I don't even know where to start."

I can only guess what's going through her head as she says this. It might feel good to offload parts of the truth and take some weight off me that's been crushing my chest for countless years, but then it hits me: I've mentioned more than I ever should. I can't let her into my world any further.

"No, I've said too much. Please don't ask me anything else. I can't have you getting caught up in all of this. You can still leave now before it's too late. I haven't said enough to land you in trouble yet." I think about how the US Marshal assigned to me taught me to never so much as say my ex's name.

Beth lowers her head in thought.

I take up her previous position and pace around. What have I done? I should have kept my damn mouth shut. What if Zach's got this place bugged somehow and is hearing everything? What if that box I've left on the kitchen bench is a microphone? He will already know there's a Beth who rents with me and that she's a student.

"I guess you're right," Beth says. "But no, I can't just leave you here. What sort of person would I be? Besides, isn't it time you called the cops or whoever looks after this kind of thing and tell them you think your ex has found you?"

"That's what I was thinking about doing before you overheard Emilio at the front door."

"Sorry."

"Don't be; I'm the one who's sorry. I shouldn't have taken you in knowing all this. It was selfish of me. I really needed the money."

Beth frowns a little as she realizes I'm right. "Yeah, I guess that wasn't the best idea but what's done is done. Besides, I know now. I can help you out of this mess."

"I doubt it," I mutter. No one can save me. Not now, not ever. I dug my grave five years ago. I've just been waiting all this time for someone to push me in.

"Come on, Karen. Let's get you some coffee. After that, I think you should call whoever it was you were going to call before I interrupted."

The coffee sounds like heaven as I wander to the sofa and take a seat. Then again, I could drink the stuff at any hour. I often had four or five cups a day to avoid sleeping as much as I could. Despite wanting to do nothing more than to hit my bed running and sleep for a month, I never manage to get in more than an hour or two before a nightmare springs me back up again.

Beth leaves me seated as she makes me an extra strong coffee with milk and sugar.

Minutes later, the brew hits my lips. I feel a calm take hold, one that's fleeting, but it's all I've got.

"So, who do you have to call about all of this?" Beth asks.

I glance up from my mug and see her all-too-eager face desperate to know more. Is this like a soap opera to her? This is my life we're talking about here. Not some twisted storyline.

"Don't worry about it," I say. "I need to speak with them on my own."

"Okay, that's fair. I only want to do what I can to hel—"

"It's fine, Beth," I interrupt. "I've got it. I'll call them. For now, I just want to enjoy my coffee." I close my eyes and bury my head into my spare hand. I don't know why I'm getting upset at Beth. She's done nothing wrong except put up with my nonsense. She shouldn't be here risking her neck like this.

I decide I need to send Beth on her way before I make the call. It's the only decent thing I can do for her.

CHAPTER ELEVEN

"I'm not going anywhere," Beth says when I explain myself to her. I try to direct her to her room to pack all of her clothing and things so she can leave, but she won't have any of it. "I told you, I'm here to help. You can't make me go."

"Yes, I can," I say, half begging. "You still have your whole life ahead of you. I will not be the one to ruin it for you now, okay?"

Beth scoffs. "What are you on about? You're what, ten years older than me at the most?"

I stop trying to push her and shrug. "Sure, I'm not much older, but I've lived hard. I've done things I shouldn't have. Trust me when I say I probably deserve this. I really do."

Beth's eyes fall to the floor. "We've all got our secrets or done crap we're not proud of. Hell, you think I haven't got any regrets in my life? If I could, I'd go back in a time machine and start over. But we can't hit a magic button and make it all fly away. We're best to admit to our failings and accept the past."

I hold the look Beth gives me, wondering what's behind those puppy dog eyes she's ashamed of. I can't imagine her living a crazy life. Maybe she wants to help me. Maybe I should let her. God knows I could use someone to lean on throughout this awful time, but if anything were to happen to her because of me...

"So, will you let me continue to help you?" she asks. "I promise you it's what I want."

I shrug at her. I can't tell if Beth is looking for her next thrill or if she would feel guilty leaving. "If you really prefer to stay, I won't stop you."

"Good, because I won't walk out on you. I couldn't live with myself if I left and later found out that your ex murdered you in the night or something insane."

We stand in the middle of the living room, staring at one another in silence to what Beth just said. Only the tick from a nearby clock in the kitchen that never holds the time well breaks through the sound of my breathing.

"So, what happens now?" Beth asks. "I mean, how do you get onto the police? Do you dial a special number?"

"Something like that. In five years, I've never had to use that option."

Beth's eyes light up to this information. She's not smiling or listening in with glee, but she seems to enjoy this on some level while showing me fear at the same time. Is this what people her age are like now? Is this how they get their kicks and enjoy new experiences? Someday I'll be a great bar story for her to tell.

"Wait," Beth says. "This person you call, were they the one who put you in this home for witness protection?"

"Not this house. I was in a witness protection apartment for about a year. Then, my contact decided enough time had passed with my ex behind bars that it was okay for me to move into a regular place and start paying rent. They found this house for me believing it to be far enough away to be safe. I'm still part of the program. Just not as desperate as I was in the beginning. At least I thought so."

"Wow," Beth says. "Just like that. One year doesn't seem all that long for them to think you are safe enough to move to a regular house, does it."

"No," I reply, remembering the day all too well when the US Marshal came to my door and sat me down to have the difficult conversation. I was told of a new family that needed the apartment ASAP and that there had been no threats made by my ex since I had helped to put him away. I tried to tell them he was biding his time and that one year wasn't enough to make such a rushed call, but they wouldn't hear it. They had to pry me from that place.

"Maybe they'll listen to you now that you've received a direct threat."

"Maybe," I say. "But a card written in Latin delivered indirectly by an unknown source isn't exactly a smoking gun."

Beth gives me a rushed smile, trying her best to reassure me things are okay, I guess.

"So what did this card say?" Beth asks. "It must be bad."

I close my eyes for a moment as I turn away from her. I don't want to see the card again or be near it.

"It's okay. You don't need to say. I thought it might help me understand better what we're dealing with here."

The tears forming in my eyes get stopped by a quick breath. I exhale and move toward the open box I left on the counter by the kitchen. As my trembling fingers unwrap the brown paper within, I realize I may have spoiled any chance of allowing evidence to be collected and analyzed. Stupid idiot. I should have known better. I guess the allure of a mysterious package was enough to draw anyone in. Besides, Emilio had covered the thing with his own DNA.

I unfold the balled-up paper that fills most of a small container and find the note still there, still waiting for a victim. Picking the card up, I see its words again and hand it over to Beth. "Do you know any Latin?"

She shakes her head. "Only what's already in everyday use. Nothing beyond that. Is that what this is? Latin?"

"Yeah. Omnia mors aequat. It means 'death makes all equal.' I studied Latin in College before I met my ex. He appreciated how much I loved the dead language and knew enough to able to whisper quotes into my ears when we were dating. It makes sense he would send me a note written in Latin with a threat. No one else knows me that well."

Beth stares at the cursive words on the card with her mouth partially open. She holds one arm tight around her body, showing me she really cares about her own life. I knew she couldn't think this was all a big joke worth staying here for. Will she second-guess her decision to stay? I won't stop her from changing her mind and leaving now.

"'Death makes all equal.' What does that mean?" she asks.

I let out an audible sigh, not wanting to elaborate the context of Zach's threat, but I have no choice. I opened this can of worms. "It's from an old poem I barely remember, but the meaning is simple. No matter who we are in life, the richest or most feared individual, down to the lowliest form of humanity, death makes us all equal. He is saying that despite him being locked up behind bars, judged as a terrible criminal while I live free out in the world, death will make us equal."

Beth exhales. "Heavy," is all she can say.

"Yes. It may not be one hundred percent clear he is threatening me, but I know exactly what he means. I'm not the first person he's ever threatened with Latin."

"What a nutcase," Beth says. "Do you think he'll send more notes?"

I stare away, already knowing the answer. My ex was always one who enjoyed spinning a narrative, especially when dealing with someone he deemed to be a problem. I turn back to Beth. "Let's hope not. Anyway, I don't have time to think about what he's got planned next. I need to make a phone call."

CHAPTER TWELVE

Beth tries to follow me into my room, knowing I'm about to make a call to the US Marshal who got assigned to my case five years ago. "I have to do this on my own," I say. "I appreciate you trying to help me through this and all, but my contact would not be happy to know I've spilled as much as I have to a person I hardly know."

"Would you get into any trouble if they found out?" she asks.

"Not exactly, but I was warned about all kinds of consequences for talking about my situation to anyone, even after I moved out of the WITSEC house."

"WITSEC?" Beth asks.

"Sorry, witness protection. Guess I still have the lingo stuck in my head. Anyway, I'll let you know how this goes." I close my bedroom door, blocking out the concern coating Beth's face. She seems to be taking this all to heart. Most people I meet her age don't hold so much empathy for their fellow person. Seeing her former roommate get stalked by some desperate guy gave her some perspective for my intense situation.

I sit on the edge of my bed and take in a deep breath. I haven't spoken to the man I am about to call, Deputy US Marshal Dustin Taylor, in over a year. Dustin used to check in on me on a monthly basis after the first twelve months. The frequency of his calls has dropped off with time down to once a year. That will change after today.

I don't make many calls on my cell. It's used to buy things online and to allow me to live vicariously through people who share their world on Facebook, Instagram, and YouTube. I have no friends or regular contacts through my phone number given the circumstances of my existence, so it doesn't matter when I swap out its sim for a special one that only Dustin has the number of.

Once a week, I go through this process in case he's called with anything of significance I need to be aware of. For the last twelve months, there has been nothing every time I load up this tiny piece of plastic. This swap will be different though. I'll be making a call to him with concerns for my life and the only other person around me that might fall victim to my ex's wrath.

How did I let this happen? Was I too careless online? Did I allow too many delivery people see my face? I'd only left the house three times in the last year. Each time I had no choice. I was careful on all three trips, wearing a hat low over my eyes and to keep to myself. No one ever followed me home or took more than a single glance in my direction.

I sigh. It doesn't matter what chain of events has led to this moment. I have no other option but to call Dustin and beg for his help. A long breath escapes my lips as I dial Dustin's number. According to the US Marshal, my sim has a special identifier that only he can understand. Via means I do not comprehend the cell's location also stays out of the hands of anyone attempting to trace the call. If ever there's a time for paranoia, it's during one of these calls.

After a series of strange sounds that must be related to the encryption process the US Marshals have in place, my cell rings out. I listen, waiting through each ring for an answer on the other end.

After five long tones blare out, I fear the worst. What if Dustin no longer has this number? What if he left the job and didn't assign another agent to my case? I shake my head on the tenth ring, wanting more than anything to hear the US Marshal's voice.

My phone cuts out. It disconnects like it's an old landline that someone has pulled from the wall. I take the cell away from my face to see my home screen staring back at me. I press redial and turn on the loudspeaker. The call doesn't connect and throws an error at me about the network. The sim should tell my cell to latch on to the strongest tower in the area, free of charge. Instead, I'm getting no signal. Not even one strong enough to connect to the emergency system.

"What the...?" I ask the empty room. I rise from my bed and pace around, both hands concentrating on my phone. "Work, dammit!" I yell as I shake the device. I hit redial and see the call fail.

Swapping my sims, I'm back on my regular plan trying to dial out. The only number I have in there that belongs to a person is Beth's. It only dawns on me now that I've never used it once. Ignoring the thought, I try calling her cell to isolate my network problem only to see the same error message.

"Damn thing. Come on." I tap frantically at the screen like it might generate a different result. Then I realize my Wi-Fi is out, along with my Bluetooth. Sweat rushes through the skin on my forehead. Something isn't right.

A small knock followed by Beth calling out confirms my thought. I yank open my bedroom door to see Beth standing there holding her cell out with confusion lining her brow.

"What is it?" I ask.

"I understand you're about to make that important call, but I thought you might want to know something weird is going on with my cell signal."

"You too?" I ask.

Beth nods. "It's like there's no reception."

I shake my head at her, unsure what this suggests until I'm slapped in the face with a memory that relates to our situation. "I know what this is," I say, eyes wide. "I've seen it before."

"What do you mean?"

I walk past Beth and move through the hallway to the living room without explanation. My mind drifts back, beyond five years ago to a time when I witnessed several bank robberies I did nothing about. Moments before a storm of chaos would come crashing down on an unsuspecting bank, my ex and his team would block out all forms of communication in the area with a short-range signal jammer. Anything that wasn't hardwired no longer seemed to function. By the time the staff in the building realized, my ex's crew had already swept in and disabled the landlines and any fail safes that could interrupt their process.

I still remember one of the first times he robbed a bank in front of me while I sat in the car and watched. In my defense, I didn't realize what was happening, but once I figured it out, I didn't do a thing to stop him. Instead, I let myself become an accessory to a federal crime all while we were supposed to be out on a date. Why didn't I walk away then? Was I too weak and compliant? Whatever the answer is, I ended up waiting until it was too late, until something awful happened.

"What do you mean?" Beth repeats, pulling me back from those days.

I shake off thoughts of the past and move up to one of the barred windows. Brushing aside a curtain enough to peek outside, I already know what will be waiting out there for me.

"What is it?" she asks.

I point out to an idling car in the street, just beyond the reach of the cameras that cover the front of the house. Smoke billows out the exhaust of a black SUV with a lone male driver. A moment later, the engine goes dead and a man in a suit climbs out. He matches the exact description of the person who paid Emilio two hundred dollars to deliver my Latin note.

I stumble backward and let the curtain fall into place as I turn to Beth with a quivering lip. My suspicions are confirmed.

"Karen?" Beth lets out.

"We're being watched."

CHAPTER THIRTEEN

I do what I can to stop myself from freaking out as I charge to my room. Beth has more questions for me. My brain can't handle answering them as I check on the one thing I hope in vain this man standing outside by his black SUV hasn't taken control over. I wiggle the mouse to my sleeping laptop and wait for the screen to activate. I log back into the system and see I don't have a Wi-Fi connection to the Internet. It's just like my cell.

"Oh God," I let out. I can't reach Dustin or call the police. I can't even contact the police online through Skype. The software throws a message at me every time I load it up, warning me that the service cannot be used to make emergency calls. I have a workaround, but it only works with a functioning Internet connection.

I feel a lump settle in my throat as I think about Skype. It reminds me of the job David will no doubt be firing me from. I can't even check my emails to see if he has torn me to pieces yet for the disastrous meeting. I was putting off the task for as long as possible. Now it would be a welcome distraction to find a message in my inbox that says I've been let go.

A second later, Beth stomps into my room with questions angering her face. "Who's that guy out there, and why is he watching us?"

I turn around from my laptop and try to focus on her question. "It's complicated," I say, holding back the fear that sits behind my words.

"Complicated? I suddenly can't use my cell for a single thing while a creepy guy hangs out the front of the house in the middle of the day and you want to give me that line."

She's angry. I don't blame her. "I wanted you to go, Beth. You should have listened."

She scoffs at me. "You didn't tell me that some weirdo would show up this soon to block our cells and Wi-Fi. You told me your ex was in prison serving a life sentence. I figured the note he sent was to scare you."

I turn away from Beth back to my laptop. "My ex doesn't screw around, but I never thought he would move this fast. I thought I had more time," I say, almost whispering.

"We should go. Just because we can't make calls or get online doesn't mean we can't jump into my Honda and head straight to the cops. Easy as that."

I face Beth and grab her by the arms. "That's a terrible idea. I won't let you risk your life and get mixed up in this. Ultimately, I don't think my ex is after you. Neither is that man out there. He's been sent here for me. You can still leave."

Beth comes further into my room, further into my sanctuary. "How do you know for certain I'm not a target just for living here?" She holds her gaze at me as her chest puffs in and out.

"I don't," I say, shaking my head. "I can't guarantee you anything, and I'm sorry. Believe me. I only wish you'd left last night while it was still an option."

Beth's eyes stay fixed and wide on mine as she tries to mouth her frustrations at me. She seems to be stuck in a combination of anger and fear. Too much to even speak a reply.

"I don't want your apology, Karen. It's too late for that. You need to do whatever it takes to fix this so we can both get the hell out of here. No one has come crashing through the front door yet, so that tells me we still have time to do something."

I take in a breath and close my eyes to center myself as best I can. When I open them again, I focus on Beth. "That man out there matches the description of the person who paid my pizza delivery guy to drop off the threatening message in a box. He has to be using a piece of equipment that jams our cell signals and the

Wi-Fi. I can't tell you what he'll do next, but I can try to create a distraction so you can take off."

Beth sighs. "Look, I realize I just came in here a minute ago demanding an end to whatever this is, but also I told you I won't leave you. Especially now. So forget it. What else you got?"

I take a step back, somewhat surprised by Beth's willingness to stay. I think about her question as my eyes fall to the crappy worn floorboards. They squeak every time Beth or I walk over them. I try my hardest to figure things out, to pull some grand idea out of nowhere, but nothing comes to mind. I raise my head and shrug.

"Nothing? You can't seriously have nothing. This is crazy." She slaps her hands to her sides.

I hold up my palms, emphasizing my expression. "I don't know what else to say."

Beth's brow squeezes in tight as she fumbles with the next words I can see are dying to come out of her mouth. She glances to the front of the house and back. "Okay, tell me then: what kind of criminal was your ex that he would send someone like that out here to make sure you can't leave home, huh?"

I hold her gaze and don't say a word.

"It's time you told me more about him, Karen. What did he do that made you testify against him?"

I shudder, not wanting to think about him or why I had to put him away in jail for life. "No, I can't mention anything else. You can still get out of whatever this is by claiming you know nothing. You didn't put my ex in prison. If I can contact him somehow, I can convince him to leave you out of this."

Beth comes in closer; both arms crossed. "That's a terrible idea. Criminals aren't known to listen to logic or reason. Now I don't know this guy the way you do, but you can't honestly believe he would let me go."

"No, he wouldn't," I say, realizing she's right again. I have to stop this denial. I have to stop my brain from trying to protect me from the truth.

"Okay, good. So we see that's not an option. There has to be a better idea to get us both out of here."

"I'm all ears," I say as if the answer is just waiting for us to find.

Beth groans a little. "There's got to be something we haven't considered. He can't have blocked us off from the world this easily."

"No, he can't," I almost whisper as a thought hits me. "I might have something. He may be jamming our signal, but there's another way we can still get online and contact the police."

"How?" Beth jumps up and down a little.

I head to my room and grab my laptop. I set it down on the coffee table and place my hands on my hips. "Our cells and Wi-Fi are blocked, but I think I can still get a wired connection on this thing to the Internet. We just need to find some cable."

CHAPTER FOURTEEN

Beth and I stand in the living room while the focused man outside continues to keep watch over the house. Not a single piece of communication has been exchanged between us. The only thing we know for certain is that he wants us to stay inside, cut off from the world. If only I could call Dustin. He'd command a cavalry of police our way and have Zach interrogated in prison. I'd love to know why now, after five years, my ex has sent a strange creep out to my home to scare the hell out of me.

"So how do we do this?" Beth asks.

I shake the thoughts out of my head and home in on the idea I have to bypass the signal jammer. "My laptop. It's an old one and still has an Ethernet port. If I find a compatible cable and connect my computer to our modem in the kitchen, I can get us online."

Beth stares at my laptop, one hand holding an elbow while the other grips her chin. "If we can get back on the web, can you call the police?"

"I know a way," I say.

"Okay. So where do you keep the Ethernet cord?" Beth asks with a smile.

"That's the problem. I'm positive I stored it all away in the small garden shed outside."

"Outside? You can't be serious." Beth groans.

"It's not something anyone uses anymore. I don't know why I even have it to begin with. By all rights, I should have thrown it out. Still, we'll check my room first for a cable as I only need about a foot of the stuff to do this. We might get lucky."

"Lucky? I doubt that word exists within this situation," Beth says. I can see her frustrations growing by the minute. Her shoulders appear to be tightening up with stress. These bizarre circumstances are new to her. I've had five years of build up to prepare for any kind of terrible outcome. Despite me coming up with a potential solution, I don't think Beth will be happy until I resolve this whole problem.

"Let's try my room. But first, we should take a peek at our friend outside. I think it's best to keep an eye on him at all times. Such a shame he's just beyond the range of my cameras, not that I can access them. Bastard must have known where to watch out for my setup."

Beth sighs as we walk across the living room to the drapery. "These people seem to know everything about you," she says. "I really think you should tell me more about them or your ex, at least."

We stop short of the curtain. "Why?" I ask.

"Because maybe I can help you to understand more. I get you see me as some dumb college student who has no real-world experience, but I might think of a way to get us out of this mess."

I feel my head swivel away as I try to dodge her words. "You'll be safer if you learn nothing about him."

"There you go again saying 'him'. I know his name is Zach. You let that slip before. Just explain what he did. It's driving me insane not knowing."

His full name flicks into my mind: Zachary Sanchez. I hate it. Every letter makes me feel sick. I never breathe those two words unless I have to, and Beth wants me to tell her why he's in prison like it doesn't make me want keel over and die.

"I can't say it," I whisper. "Please don't force it out of me. I promised the US Marshal I wouldn't reveal anything about him. I shouldn't have told you a single thing about any of this. I should have left the second I got that package. I'm so sorry."

Beth stares at me, anger across her brow as she holds her gaze at me. She must think I'm the worst person in the world. But as suddenly as her rage comes through, it dissipates. Her face softens.

"No, I'm sorry, Karen. I don't know why I want to know what happened. It changes nothing. I guess I'm just losing it."

"It's okay," I say with a lowered head. "This is what he does to people. That's why I think you're safer off not knowing who he is. I wish every day of my life I'd never met him."

We share a moment of silence. I can only hope Beth and I have reached an understanding with Zach. I don't like thinking about him let alone talking about the bastard who ruined my future.

"Let's see what this weirdo outside is up to before we go hunting for my Ethernet cable," I say.

Beth is ahead and takes the last few steps toward the window. She brushes the curtain open enough for the two of us to spy through a smallish gap at the SUV parked near the house. There's no real need to be subtle anymore. He knows we're here. We know he's out there.

"What the hell?" Beth blurts.

I rush over, not liking the sound of her voice. "What is it?" I ask trying to focus.

"He's gone."

"What do you mean gone?"

"Look."

I squeeze my head around a bar and squint my eyes to the SUV to see that no one is standing beside it. "Where did he go?"

"I don't know," Beth says. "Maybe he wasn't watching us. Maybe we've just been letting ourselves get paranoid for nothing."

"But he fits the description Emilio gave me. You overheard that conversation. That guy was a perfect match."

"I know," Beth says, her voice deflated. "Just trying to convince myself this isn't happening. What do we do now?"

I grab my cell from my pocket. "Our phones are still being jammed. He must have left the device on before he walked off. Maybe that's all he was supposed to do. Then again, his car is still here."

"He mustn't be too far away then," Beth says.

"I guess not." I walk away from the curtain and turn to the side door that leads to the backyard. Focusing on Beth, I recognize she already knows what I will say next.

"You can't be serious?" she says.

I nod. "I wish I wasn't, but I think it's time we headed outside to grab that cable."

CHAPTER FIFTEEN

I stand by the side door and unlock its four deadbolts. Installed here is the same over-the-top configuration as on the front. I figured if someone wanted to break in, they will try this entrance over the front. This side door is more private. It's just a simple matter of jumping over the fence into a narrow pathway that runs along the length of the house. From there, no one can see you.

Of course, I have a camera sitting above the door, ready to record anyone stupid enough to try such a move, but without the Internet, I'd have no clue until after the fact if anyone had trespassed.

It makes me seem a little nuts to most people, having such a paranoid setup, but I've had to accept extra precautions to survive.

"Are you sure about this?" Beth asks. "We have no idea where he is out there. What if he's just around the corner waiting for one of us to come outside?"

I feel a jitter in my hands. I stop to take a breath and calm my nerves in any way possible. "If I see him, I'll race inside. Don't you worry. Besides, this is the perfect time to do this. He probably thinks we're going to run out the front door and not the rear."

Beth runs a hand through her blonde hair. "I guess that makes sense. But what if he catches you? He might have a gun on him. Do you think he'd shoot?"

I shudder thinking about this as I hate guns. It's not that I'm against anyone owning them or anything political, I just have a bad history with them, one I never like to think about.

"Well?" Beth asks, growing impatient.

"If he wanted to kill us, he'd have done so already. My ex is taking his time with this to torture me. We're alive because he wants us to be."

"Oh, great," Beth says, her face drooping with anguish. "Another thing to drive me crazy."

"Sorry. I didn't mean to be so blunt, but don't worry. I will get you out of this, okay? I promise."

Beth half smiles. I have no idea if we'll make it out of here, but I'll do what I can to make sure nothing foul happens to her while I still can. Unlike me, she deserves none of the hell Zach has planned for me. "Wish me luck," I say.

"Wait," Beth says. "What's the idea here?"

I place a hand on the doorknob and close my eyes. "Simple. I head outside and try to find the cable. The shed isn't far from the dead side of the house. You stay in here by the door and hold it open. If you see or hear anything bad happen, you slam it shut and lock it, okay?" I turn away from her and twist the handle.

"Wait," Beth says again.

I glance over my shoulder. "What is it?"

"Aren't you afraid to go outside?"

I release my grip on the knob and feel my neck tense up. "Yes. Terrified."

"So how are you going to do this then?"

"I'll figure it out. I have to. Zach can't do this to us."

Beth shakes her head, doubt written across her forehead. "That won't be enough. Despite only living here for three months, I know you. Like you said, you get everything you need shipped in. You work from home in the study. You're basically an agoraphobic. How long has it been since you last left the house?"

"I'm not agoraphobic," I say, shame filling my voice. "I've just had to change my lifestyle to survive. That's all this has ever been."

Beth raises her brow with a tilted head. "Don't avoid the question."

"I'll be okay, Beth. Trust me," I say, not having an answer for her.

"What if you collapse? What if you freak out?"

"I won't." I grab the knob and twist. A crack of daylight floods through, expanding as I open the door further until it's enough for me to squeeze out of a slight gap. Beth follows me and holds it steady, standing half in and half out of the house. "I still think this is a bad plan," she says behind me.

She's trying her hardest to talk me out of this idea. I can't tell if it's out of concern or if she's afraid. "What else can we do?" I ask without looking back. I feel the day's dry heat swarm over and pull me down the two steps that rise to the side door as I move further outside.

When my feet hit the ground, an odd sensation overwhelms me as I think about how easy it used to be to do this once upon a time. I've taken something as simple as shuffling a foot outdoors into my backyard for granted.

I creep along the gravel pathway, ever aware of the crunching sound that my feet make with each step. I wouldn't notice such a thing, but in this agonizing moment, I can hear each of my footfalls as if I were wearing heavy combat boots.

I reach the end of the house and lean my hand out to grab the corner of the wall. I need to creep up to the edge as much as possible to take a peek around the side to where the small shed lies. It holds mostly rusted gardening equipment that came with the home that I will never use as long as I'm the tenant here.

On one of my rare trips outside, I noticed the shed and investigated. I remember finding it full of space for me to store junk I was too stupid to get rid of. On top of my other issues, I have a hard time throwing anything out. Just a real winner right here.

Focusing, I grip the edge of the brick house and pull myself up to the corner. With as much calm as I can find within, I take a quick glance around the backyard. Nothing but half-dead patchy grass meets my eye. A broken-down Toyota Tacoma sits in the grass with flat tires. The owner of the house neglected to remove the pickup from the property long before I moved in. I hate the sight of the decaying wreck.

With a full sweep of the area, I locate the garden shed sitting only a few quick steps away. Next, I need to find the courage to move out from the safety of the narrow pathway into the open yard. It's not a big space, but it seems to feel like it's the size of a football field.

My heart thumps hard against my chest as I pull myself around the corner. I scrape my body over the rough brickwork and edge along one step at a time until I reach the shed. It leans against the building at an angle. It's another example of the neglect ever present on the property.

I make it to the shed and place my hand on its rusty handle only to freeze when I hear the crunching sound of gravel being stepped on from the other side of the house. I pin myself against the wall as hard as I can when I should be running back to the side door inside.

The crunching grows louder, freezing me where I stand. The footsteps are coming toward me. He'll be in the backyard in a matter of seconds.

CHAPTER SIXTEEN

"Come on," I whisper to myself as the footsteps continue approaching me from the opposite side of the house. They have to belong to him—the man in the suit. Who else could it be? I listen in to his dress shoes scuffing hard against the gravel, kicking stones along as he goes. Why is he wearing a suit? The outfit makes him stand out in this street. Does he want to appear like some wannabe professional hitman? Has he seen too many movies?

The footsteps grow louder, forcing more dumb questions into my mind. Is he working to find a path through to the house somehow, or is he trying to see what options we have for escape? Either way, I have to get indoors before it's too late.

Move, I tell myself.

I edge back, pushing myself along the wall and away from the shed that potentially holds the Ethernet cable Beth and I sorely lack. Without it, we're not only stuck inside this place, cut off from communication with the rest of the world, but we could be sacrificing our only chance of surviving this ordeal.

I realize a second later that I've left my escape inside a moment too long and have no option but to rush over to the small garden shed and use it as cover. I press myself as far into it as I can, squishing my face into a corner that consists of cool metal on one surface and dusty brickwork on the other. Will it be enough to hide me? All he'll have to do is move further into my section of the yard to see me. He'll catch me trying to slip away and have no alternative but to kill me where I stand. Beth will be next, leaving no witnesses to this daytime slaughter.

I can't help these kinds of thoughts. I could never put it past Zach to have me killed. Why though, didn't that thought stop me from taking Beth in? My death, I can handle. But being responsible for an innocent girl's demise breaks my heart in two.

I hold my breath as the man comes around the corner from the gravel lane to the dirt patch of a backyard that should be lined with grass. He stops. I can hear him breathing and sniffing out loud as he takes in the terrible view. Is he looking for me? Is he learning how much privacy he has if he needs to load up our dead bodies into his fancy SUV? Whatever he's up to, it's distracting him from finding me.

I stay quiet and still, not wanting to reveal my whereabouts, but the metal of the small shed buckles inward, pulling me with it. I do what I can to let it flex without making too much noise, but the inevitable crack sounds out. My face slams forward to the new indent I've made by pressing too heavily against the material. There's no way he didn't hear me.

My heart pounds so hard, I swear I feel it flow through to the shed. My pulse rattles in my ear as I attempt to contain my breathing. All I want to do is let out a cry and gulp in all the dry air around me. Two feet scuff in my direction.

I'm dead. This is how I die. After five years of hell, I'm about to meet my end. Maybe it's for the best.

His cell chirps out loud with a call, ceasing his movement. A standard ringtone. The guy answers with a "yeah" and listens to the person on the other end.

Several moments of silence pass by without either one of us moving. Who is he talking to? Is it Zach? He must have the ability to bypass the jammer.

"Understood," he says. With no further explanation, the man turns back the way he came and walks off. He continues from the dirt patch to the gravel. The sound of his refined steps as they progress away from the garden shed allows me to breathe louder than before.

I feel my body slide down the brick pattern of the house as I move my face away from the walls. A lungful of terrified air shudders its way out a second later. What the hell just happened?

After too long a time, I pull myself together and start for the door on the other side of the shed. I don't have a second to waste. I know the door will creak the second I operate the handle, but I have to find that cable.

I pull open the garden shed with slight force and discover a mess and a half greet me. Why couldn't I have left it organized with the box I need sitting in an easy-to-access place? Instead, with enough crap in my way that I have no choice but to make noise, I grab the box I know has the Ethernet cable inside. An outdoor broom topples over my head and clangs hard against the wall of the shed. I stop pulling at the carton and freeze. My luck has run out for sure, not that I had much to begin with.

I hear his footsteps crunch again over the gravel, faster than before.

CHAPTER SEVENTEEN

"Come on. Run. Just grab it and run," I say to myself. My back is exposed to the world outside of the garden shed as I hear the distant sound of footsteps approaching me again. This time, they are determined and focused.

"Come on," I repeat, my eyes sealed shut. I have to leave or stay. Run or hide in this tiny metal box. Both ideas have plenty of potential for failure. It seems to be the only thing I'm good at.

"Screw this," I whisper. My eyes fly open as I bend down and scoop up the carton I think contains the Ethernet cord I so badly need. I feel the contents of the container smash around in my arms as I stumble out from the shed. I accidentally leave the door wide open, making it clear I was just here, trying to find a desperate way to save both myself and Beth from whichever psycho-for-hire Zach sent after me.

I run over the dirt-patch lawn to the narrow pathway around the dead side of the house. Beth hangs out of the opening, waving me in. She knows he must be right behind me from the noise I made looking for the Ethernet cabling. Either that or he is right behind me. I'm not turning around to find out.

We spill back into the living room together. I throw the box to the floor and spin back to slam the side door shut and apply its four deadbolts one after the other. If I could pull the refrigerator down in front of it, I would.

A surge of adrenaline courses through me, powering me on, giving me a strength I'd forgotten all about. I can't help remembering one time when Zach took me along for a ride in one of his cars as he and his associates robbed a bank before my eyes. I knew what they were planning on doing, but I didn't realize it would pull me into their world with such force.

When Zach sped off from the cops at speeds I'd never experienced in his modified vehicle, I felt as if I was about to die. I thought the police would force us straight into a tree or a power line pole, killing us instantly for daring to flee. But we got away. Zach had it all worked out. He knew where to go and what to do. He escaped the police chase with hundreds of thousands of dollars sitting on my lap where he'd placed it. I should have left him then. I should have seen through the lifestyle he was seeking to entice me with, but I was too young and naive to think for myself.

Well, I will not be that ignorant person anymore and let him win this easily. I look at Beth's shaking hands as she clutches her cell. I could picture her struggling to search for a signal while I was gone. Her fingers continue to jitter as I feel a steadiness overwhelm me.

"Did he see you?" she asks.

"I don't know. I could hear him coming for me. He was scoping out the backyard. Probably trying to find another way in."

"You think?"

"Had to be. He realizes we won't run," I say as I conclude in my head.

"What makes you think that?" Beth asks as her hands steady.

"Simple. He knows we've spotted him out there. He's not trying to hide his presence from us if he's walked around the back of the house without a care in the world."

"Great. This guy has confidence on his side. Should make killing us a whole lot easier."

I look down at the box. "I won't let that happen, Beth," I say. I squat and tilt the cardboard over to the correct way up. "I've been running from Zach for too long to let him keep doing this to me. I won't let him ruin another young life."

Beth steps back from me as I pry the box open with both hands. She must feel my sincerity as I bare my soul in front of her unlike I've been able to for so long. If only I could explain myself in full and give her the absolute truth. I decide in the moment if I can save Beth from whatever this is and survive Zach's control, I will tell her everything about my past. All of it.

"Did you at least find the cable?" Beth asks.

"I think so," I say. "I know I shoved it in here a few years ago as a backup. I never thought it would be for something so crazy as this." Old tech falls from the box in the form of items that will never be demanded again. Dusty oversize hard drives and their power adapters impede the Ethernet cable I need more than anything else in this house.

"Here we go." I find one end of the cord and tug it through and out of the carton. From memory, the cable is too long. I don't know why I thought I'd need so much.

"It's a mile long," Beth jokes.

"I know," I chuckle. "Almost got the damn thing out. Just have to locate the—" I stop myself short when I find the end of the cable. "Perfect. Okay, Beth, take this and run it out to the modem in the kitchen. Put it into one of the spare ports that has the word LAN above it. I'll plug the other end into my laptop."

"And then we'll be back online?"

"Simple as that." I say as I run the cable toward my laptop. Beth moves in the opposite direction to the kitchen. "There's no way in hell that guy out there can block a wired connection," I say. "Zach probably figured I wouldn't have the capability to work out such a thing. He guessed wrong."

I reach my laptop and see it is still offline with multiple programs trying to bug me to access the web. What did we ever do on computers before the Internet came to be? I find the Ethernet port on my workstation and plug in the cable, giving the port a quick blow beforehand to remove any dust.

"Okay, Beth. I'm in. How about you?" I pause, waiting in anticipation for her to confirm she's done her part. I look back to my screen and see I'm still disconnected from the rest of the world.

"Karen. We may have a problem."

"What?" I ask. "Don't tell me you're too young to work out where to plug it in. This is just gold." I rush to her and move toward the modem, seeing Beth standing over the device like she's stumbled upon some ancient ruins. "Kids today," I tut. I feel so old suddenly despite my age.

"It's not that," Beth says, almost at a whisper.

The pit of my stomach turns into knots when I realize something is wrong. I stand beside Beth and spot her holding a section of the cable near the end by the plug. A great big chunk of insulation around the wiring is missing. Half of the wiring below has been severed. How did I miss this before?

Beth turns to me with tears in her eyes. "Can you fix this?"

I think the damage is most likely caused by rats and shake my head. "No."

"You must be able to. We could try to twist the wires back into place. There's probably something inside this carton that—"

Beth stops talking when she picks up the box and sees the same thing as me. Several holes exist in the corners where the vermin have chewed their way in. My eyes transition to the damaged Ethernet cord. There's no way in hell I can use this long useless cable to connect to the Internet now.

Beth and I stare at one another in silence as I realize how trapped we truly are.

CHAPTER EIGHTTEEN

"What do we do?" Beth rattles at me for the third time in a row as I search through my room for an Ethernet cable. My laptop now sits on my desk, still disconnected from the web. I still can't believe the cord I risked my life to retrieve is broken. It's like someone knew I would need it and destroyed it. That, or the more likely explanation being vermin had gotten into the shed and chewed their way into the unprotected box. The truth didn't matter. Without the cord, we can't get online and call for help, be it the police or Dustin.

"Seriously, Karen, what the hell are we going to do? We can't keep searching for this damn thing. We need to act and take charge and—"

"And what?" I yell, interrupting as I face her. "We both know that guy out there has to be armed. Criminals don't exactly show up to places without some sort of weapon. Plus, the second he catches one of us, he'll pit us against each other. I've seen it before."

Beth frowns. "What is that supposed to mean?"

"Nothing," I say, twisting back to a box of junk under my desk. I shouldn't tell her about the techniques Zach and his team used to lure bank managers out from their secured offices.

"Karen? Please don't ignore me. It doesn't take a genius to realize Zach was up to no good for him to be put away for life. I also know that he must have pulled you along for the ride in order for you to testify against him, so why can't you tell me more?"

"I already told you that the less—"

"Enough," she spits out. "I've been patient for too long. Not only that, I've risked my life staying here with you. Don't you think it's time you let me in on even just a slither of the truth?"

I tilt my head to the side. The random piece of junk I hold in one hand falls back into the box I'm searching through. I shake my head, knowing she's somewhat right. Pushing myself from the floor, I pull out my cell and check the signal again, praying that my smartphone picks up a nearby tower so I can avoid telling Beth more. But no matter how desperate I am for the jammer to stop working, it's obvious that we're still cut off by the man lurking about our property.

"Karen?" Beth reiterates.

I let a sigh escape my parted lips as I face her. "Zach was a bank robber. I knew that about him when we first properly met. He didn't force me to be a part of his world; I let myself fall into it. I thought about going to the police to have him arrested many times, but I fell victim to his charm and allowed my brain to tell me we weren't doing anything wrong. Zach and his crew were ripping off large chain store banks that were richer than they deserved to be. Each outlet had insurance to cover what got stolen. No personnel in the banks were ever harmed. At least not until one night when things grew out of control." I glance up to Beth's horrified face. "I had no choice but to have him put away for life by testifying against him in court. I'll never forget that look in his eyes when he knew I had turned against him."

Beth stares at me, her mouth half open and arms crossed. "No way. A bank robber? I didn't know people still did that."

"It's not an easy career. I remember Zach always said he had to go for the big banks only. The smaller ones weren't worth the time. But the bigger the bank, the greater the risk. I swore I'd see him gunned down in the street on the news one day, but it never happened."

Beth walks further into my room and takes a seat in a spare office chair I have tucked in the corner. Her arms remain crossed over her chest as she shakes her head. Without looking at me, she asks an obvious question. "Did you ever rob any of the banks?"

"Not exactly. I was like a willing observer who waited in the car. Occasionally, I posed as a customer and whispered into a hidden radio to let them know if any of the staff were about to panic. Deep down I knew what we were doing was terrible and that I was just as bad as them. I chose to be part of his outfit until it was too late."

Beth leans down. I already know what she will ask me next, but I wait to hear it. "What happened? What did he do to cause you to turn against him the way you did?"

My eyes drop to the box of junk. I try to hold back the tears building up, but they fall from my face to the floor, each weighing a thousand pounds. "There's not much to tell you other than I deserve what's happening right now. But you sure as hell don't. I wish I could make that man out there understand and let you go."

Beth doesn't say a word. She no longer presses me for more. I've stunned her into silence with my pathetic existence and the terrible things I'd become a part of. Her life is at risk because I allowed her to rent a room from me. What was I thinking?

"What was his full name?" she asks me suddenly.

"Why?" I ask, not looking up.

"Maybe I've heard of him before. Like I said, maybe there's something about Zach I could use to stop this. I recognize it's a long shot, but—"

"I can't say his full name. I swore I would never talk about my past, and I've already revealed too much." I squeeze my eyes closed and hit the side of my head with my palm. No matter how hard I hit though, it doesn't erase the pain.

"It's just a name," Beth says. "Nothing else. Maybe it will do you good to say it."

I stare up at her and say what I'm thinking. I can't help myself. "His name will never sound like anything other than poison."

CHAPTER NINETEEN

For the moment, we sit tight. The man in the suit hasn't made a move on us, and we haven't come up with anything worth doing in return. Beth stays close by in my room, sitting on my office chair while I finish turning the space upside down. I keep searching for a working Ethernet cable to distract myself from the painful things I revealed to Beth. I know I shouldn't have said a word to her about Zach, but I couldn't help myself. What must she think of me?

I've been on my own for too long. Even when I had other renters in, I never spoke to them beyond what was necessary. We didn't get to know one another the way I have with Beth. She attempted to be friendly with me from day one despite me giving her nothing in return. She wore me down over a short time to the point where I was happy to see her arrive home. Now I've told her too much. I kept things business-as-usual with any tenants for a reason, but she found a path in, and I have to say, it felt good to let some of my cold past out even if I didn't reveal all. Not yet anyway.

Beth has stopped asking for a solution to our impossible problem. Instead she sits on my office chair, spinning it around ninety degrees left and right. Her face remains blank and helpless. Has she given up? Surely not. We may be trapped in here, but we can't let the darkness in until we are truly screwed. There's still time to do something. It's not over.

What are you afraid of? Beth's question now seems to hit home harder than it ever has before. And not only to me, but to her own self too. She is close to breaking point and we haven't yet begun to be challenged. I know Zach. There's more on the way. More hell to be paid. This petty man doesn't let go of his grudges so easily. Unfortunately, he also has a flair for the dramatic.

"We have to get out of here," Beth mutters. "We have to."

"I know," I say as I walk out of my room and through the hallway.

A moment later, I reach the front window and slide the curtain across without care. The man is back in his old spot, now sitting inside his large SUV, staring straight at me. This man's glare is so intense it goes beyond professional. He seems determined to complete what Zach has paid him to do. How much did Zach pay him for that little extra? How much is my life worth? Will he get a bonus too for dealing with Beth? Or is she not important enough to bother with?

"I'm serious," Beth calls out. "If we don't, he'll come for us. And that'll be it. We'll be forgotten about and fade away into nothing."

I sense the desperation in her voice and head back to my room. She has possibly never considered that one day she will die. One day, her heart will no longer pump blood, her brain will fail to carry thoughts, and her lungs will stop drawing in air. She will cease to exist. I guess it's a lot for any of us to fathom.

"Why do you say that?" I ask as I reach the doorway. "You're a student in her prime. I'm confident you have more friends than I've ever had in my entire existence. People would notice if something happened to you. You wouldn't be forgotten."

"Maybe, but for every minute that passes I feel less and less convinced we'll get through this. What if I die before I've lived my life? I can't die this young."

I move into the room and walk over to Beth. Her question runs through me like a hot knife through butter, making my hands tremor. I sit on my bed and try to control the weakness overpowering me. I have nothing to quell such questions.

"How did he find you?" Beth asks. "Do you wonder what happened, like what led to him locating you?"

I hadn't thought about that until now. More damning things have been clouding my mind. I lean away from her. Why would I dwell on something so pointless? Zach knows where we are. He's got us zeroed in and surrounded by one man. Knowing the path taken to smoke me out from hiding doesn't seem all that appealing, but maybe I should know. Maybe it will reveal a mistake made or show me an assumption Zach has come to from his prison cell. I could discover the bad link in his chain by seeing what he had to do to find me.

"I'll need to think about it," I say to Beth, sinking back into my bed. My brain races over my strict boring routine and the few people I've interacted with during the last few months and beyond that could have led to Zach finding me. Nothing comes to mind.

I'm always careful and methodical in my ways. All I can imagine is that Zach hired some elite private investigator to spend months and months going from one slim lead to the next until he found me. Either that, or someone in the witness protection program got paid just the right amount of money to allow Zach to find my location. I shudder at the thought if the latter is true, but Dustin would never do such a thing.

I look to Beth. "I honestly can't tell you. I haven't noticed anything out of the ordinary. The only way I stay hidden is by keeping to a strict routine. All I can guess is maybe he got to someone high up enough in the US Marshal's department to get my address."

"Surely not," Beth replies, shock registering in her eyes. "Those people take their job seriously. I doubt a splash of fast cash could sway them."

Beth's words set me at ease. I even smile a little. "That's good to know. I'd hate to think my contact would ever place me in harm's way for a few dollars. So, do you know someone in the Marshals?"

"No, but my brother is a police officer. He's older than me. I know how incorruptible he is. He would never use his position like that, so I have to figure a US Marshal would have an even higher standard."

I continue to smile at Beth. "I guess you're right, and it's nice to see how much you trust your brother."

Beth pauses for a moment. "I have to. He's family. We grew up together. I have to believe I understand him better than anyone else I know."

I think about my brother. He passed ten years ago of a brain aneurysm. There he was at the peak of his young adult life at twenty-five, training to qualify for the Olympic swimming team when he one day collapsed into a heap by the pool. The doctors informed us he died before his head hit the ground. Of course, to make my witness relocation work, my parents had to be told I was dead. The world had to believe I was killed in a car accident so I could go into hiding.

My poor parents think they have no children left. What would it be like to go through the hardship of raising two kids from birth to adulthood only to see them die at the peak of their lives? I shudder at the thought.

Some days I sit on Dad's Facebook page, seeing what he and Mom are up to, hovering my mouse over the message button. Would they accept what I'd done if I told them the truth about all of this? It's a lot to swallow at once, even on a good day.

"Are you hungry?" Beth asks.

My head shifts up. "Not overly, but I should eat something, I guess."

"Let's go make some sandwiches. Who knows how long this guy wants to keep us locked up in here like this."

CHAPTER TWENTY

I don't offer any suggestions to Beth's rhetorical question. Zach seems to be trying to amplify my anxiety as much as he can by keeping us trapped inside. How long do we have left before the final order comes through? At this stage, I almost want Zach to get it over with. Then again, if I survive alongside Beth, it will be the greatest thing in the world to know I got away from Zach because he took too long toying with me. I have to hold on to some hope.

We walk out from my bedroom to the living area. Beth gets to work on the sandwiches in the kitchen while I lean on the edge of the sofa. She's made food for me before and seems to be quite capable of whipping up a wide variety of flavorful meals. It's refreshing to see someone her age with that kind of knowledge and ability. I've had a few tenants come through who survive on nothing but microwaved meals and DoorDash. The latter seems to be the beginning of a generation that won't ever be able to take care of itself. Instead, hard-working individuals looking to supplement their income will be forced to solve their problems for them.

I choose a seat on the sofa and place my head back. It's early in the afternoon and I still don't grasp why Zach has done this during the day. Is it to prove that no time is safe, that he doesn't have to wait for the cover of darkness to strike? I close my eyes and try to quiet down my thoughts. I don't need the constant noise asking questions that cannot be answered.

"Here you go," Beth says to my side.

I open my eyelids and roll over to take what appears to be a perfect sandwich. "Thank you," I say, not knowing what's in it.

At this point, I don't care and would eat two slices of bread with dirt between them.

"I had some leftover turkey," Beth says. "I hope it's okay."

My mouth is already too full for me to answer so I give her a quick thumbs up to show her my approval. I realize how rude I am sometimes. I often wonder who between us is more mature.

Beth stays standing as she chews. I don't think she can handle sitting right now. The stress gripping her neck muscles stands out. She's tried her hardest to hide her fear away from me, but I sense it in every step she takes.

Beth paces around as she eats, covering the small space of the living room in no time. It isn't the nicest house to be trapped in given its miniature size. I almost want to grab her by the waist and plant her butt down on the sofa so she relaxes a little. It could be hours before Zach makes another move.

Stepping up to the curtain we've used to spy on the man in the suit, Beth stops short and squints through the slight side gap of the window we should have been using to be more subtle to check outside.

"You can't be serious?" she says, slamming her plate down onto a small side table that sits by the window. It clatters about the surface without breaking. I jump to my feet and almost stumble as I rush over to see what all the fuss is about.

"What is it?" I half whisper as I reach the shade.

Beth pulls the dusty aged cloth of the curtain back so I can look through and see what's caused her to yell out. I almost faint when I discover what's got her so rattled.

"What do you think this means?" Beth asks me.

With my mouth open, I stare outside to see no man in a suit or the SUV he's used to spy on us with. He's gone again.

CHAPTER TWENTY-ONE

I'm the one pacing around the living room while my sandwich remains half eaten. Beth keeps looking outside in case Zach's man returns. We don't understand why he left or when he's coming back.

I think about Zach locked up in his cell and wonder what he is playing at by sending his gun-for-hire away yet again. Is it a test? Or did the guy have to go?

"Should we make a run for it?" Beth asks, her voice shaking a little.

We've checked our cells and Wi-Fi again. Both remain blocked, meaning the device this man has been using on us is still around. He's hidden it away just to be safe while he screws with our minds from a distance.

"Karen? Please, say something."

"I don't know what to tell you. This could all be a way to lure us out from the safety of the house like before."

"Dammit," Beth mutters. "Wait, how can you be so sure?"

My mouth stays shut. I have no idea what this all means. Instead, I focus on trying to not let the overwhelming number of thoughts kick in and take over.

Beth stops keeping watch outside and stares at me with her serious face. "I seriously think we should make a break for it. We could call the police the second we're clear of the area."

My eyes drop to the floor. "What if he is waiting to strike just out of sight?"

Beth moves toward me, raising my head. "We can do this. We can run straight out of this dump and down the street with our cells out. I'll call the cops while you call your contact."

I give her a weak smile. "What if he gets one of us though?"

"He won't if we move fast enough."

I shake my head. "This could backfire. I'm not going to see you hurt because of me."

"You won't. But if we stay here, you'll see us both hurt or worse."

She's right, I realize. We can't keep hiding like this. We have to do something while we still can.

I stare at Beth as she pulls her cell out of her pocket and tries to get a signal again. "It's still dead in here. We will be too if we don't go now." She edges her way closer to the door.

"Maybe not," I say as I see the answer right in front of my face. I close in on Beth and grab her by the wrists. "I know what to do."

"You do?"

I nod.

Beth's eyes go wide. "Tell me."

I take in a breath, ready for some backlash. "I'm going to run outside and find a signal on my cell to call the police while you stay safe in here."

Beth shakes her head, screwing up her brows at me. "No, you can't do that. Not by yourself. After everything you've told me about Zach, you have to know that's a terrible idea. You're not sacrificing yourself to save me."

"I thought you wanted to make a break for it."

"Together, I do. Not apart. We'd have more chance of getting away if we work as one."

I keep her gaze as I contemplate sneaking outside the second her back is turned. I could dash as fast as my legs can take me and call 911 the minute I clear the signal jammer, but I fight off such an idea. At least for the moment.

The jammer can't have that great of a range. If the block extends too far beyond my home, the neighbors would have noticed by now that their devices had been acting up. Technicians would have been called to work out the problem. Those people wouldn't have taken long after someone made an inspection to notify the authorities and send out a welcoming committee of police to root out the source of the illegal jammer.

"We need to stand together, Karen. Either we both go or we both stay. You choose."

I pause for a second, not saying a word. "I guess you're right. Now isn't the time to do anything so crazy."

"No, it's not. So what's it going to be?"

I take a minute to consider my options and resolve to stick to my original thought. "We stay. Whatever his move is out there, I don't trust it. This has to be a lure to draw us out into the open. It has to be."

Beth shows her understanding without anger and interlocks my elbow. "Okay. You know your ex better than anyone else. Seeing as we're staying, why don't you take a seat on the sofa and try to relax."

"Relax, huh? That's a good one. I can't even eat. This day couldn't get any worse if it tried." Beth guides me to the sofa. I comply and sit down. Maybe she's right. Our only way out of this is by sticking together. But if only one of us is to make it out, I want it to be the someone who deserves to live. That's not me.

"I'll be back in a tick. I'm just going to grab my cell charger. I forgot to plug this thing in last night," Beth says.

"Okay," I say as she leaves, thinking about how Beth came home reasonably carefree despite having an argument with her parents. Now I've trapped her in here while Zach pays someone to hover around the house no one is supposed to know about. What if something happens to her and the last thing she did with her parents was have an argument. I can't have that weighing me down along with everything else.

A few moments later, Beth reappears with her charger and plugs it in by the power socket that sits near the kitchen. "Still no signal. I don't know why I bother checking anymore."

"It can't be helped," I say, pulling my cell out of my pocket. "I check every couple of minutes like a crazy person."

"It's hard not to though, isn't it," Beth adds. "We're so dependent on these things we can't go a day without them. My cell lives within a few feet of me twenty-four hours a day. I feel sick if it's even in the next room over. God, I can't imagine how many notifications I'll have waiting for me if this asshole ever turns off that jammer."

I give Beth a faint smile. My cell might as well have its signal blocked all the time. I'd still have the same number of people trying to contact me or tag me on social media. I pull my gaze away from her as the thought sinks in.

How much have I missed out on over the last five years? How many relationships have I never had? What experiences have I forgone to stay alive? I can't call this survival when the only friend I have in the world is a fellow housemate I've known for three months.

Beth is the only one I've let into my life in any manner. I've never felt comfortable enough with anyone else. But even then, she doesn't know the real me. She wouldn't want to. The true me deserves to have this paid killer come smashing through the door to end my miserable existence once and for all.

"Why don't you take a nap," Beth suggests, cutting me out of my dark thoughts.

"Uh, no, it's okay. I'll manage."

"No you won't. I can see you haven't slept all night. You need to recuperate."

"I know I do, but what about him out there? How do I sleep with that going on? We have no idea where this guy even is."

"Simple," Beth says, smiling. "I'll keep watch. The second he shows up, or anything else happens, I'll rock you awake. I promise."

I shake my head and let out a sigh. A yawn finds its way out of my face, causing me to rub my eyes like a small child. "Okay, I guess."

"No need to thank me," Beth says with a laugh.

"Thank you," I reply, "for everything. Seriously, you've been so amazing today. I mean, I wish you didn't have to go through all of this, but I'm glad you are here."

Beth's smile drops. She's all too aware of the danger lurking outside the house. I hope my reminder hasn't shaken her too much.

"We'll pull through this," I whisper. "We have to." I settle down into the sofa and close my eyes. Before I know it, I'm on my side with a blanket Beth has settled over my body. She disappears in a sleepy blur and returns with a pillow from my room. The comfortable thickness of the cushion is placed ever so carefully under my head, maximizing my comfort.

Sleep soon catches me and drags me down.

"Sleep," Beth says.

CHAPTER TWENTY-TWO

My nightmares seem so real. Some nights, I have a lot of trouble distinguishing reality from the haze of images that wreak havoc on my brain while I'm asleep. I've had this one in particular before. Every time I think I'm rid of the damn thing it comes back. And despite being aware I'm in a dream, there's little I can do to convince myself that the world I'm in isn't absolute. It's like walking through a house haunted by spirits when you don't believe in ghosts.

I'm sitting in a luxurious car at night with Zach as we cruise down a dark highway. The city looms in the background with its bright lights. I guess it's somewhere near LA, the prime hunting ground of Zach's group. We are speeding along with nowhere to go, but no matter how fast we drive, the city keeps its distance as if we will never reach it.

We pull into a gas station that looks to be the only thing lit up in the area, but we don't need a drop of fuel. The tank is full. Zach appears distant as if I'm losing him. He won't look in my direction or react when I nudge him. Normally, we'd be laughing with one another, bathing in a carefree arrogance we couldn't shake until he grabbed me and threw me against the car to make out. But the thrill is missing. The spark is gone. He's had enough of me.

From this point on, things take a turn as I move toward the gas station alone. A foreign object weighs my hand down like a lump of steel. I take so long to get inside the store, but once I do, all I see is darkness and a lone figure standing ahead, creeping near.

A single shot from Zach's gun rings out loud in my ears. The person ahead breaks into pieces and falls apart. The world as I know it caves down overhead, forcing me further and further down into the dark until I recognize it's not concrete and steel weighing me down; it's blood.

I snap awake on the sofa in a pool of sweat. My eyes take a moment to focus on where I am, but I remember Beth saying she would keep watch out the window in case Zach's man tries to attack us. I half sit up on my elbows and understand she's not doing as planned. Panic sweeps in. The tiny hairs on the back of my neck prick up as I feel another human being right behind me. I scramble forward and spin around to see Beth standing where my head was resting only moments ago.

"Whoa, Karen. Are you okay? I didn't mean to wake you."

"It's fine," I say as I absorb the rest of my surroundings. "What were you doing there anyway?"

"I came from the bathroom. Sorry, I had to go. I was trying to walk past quietly, but I bumped into the sofa like an idiot."

"No harm done," I mumble as I grab at my forehead and rub it over and over to massage the headache that has now settled at the front of my brain. The pain seems to multiply by the hour.

"How did you sleep?" she asks me.

"Okay, I guess. I could use a few more hours."

"Really? You've been out for over seven."

That's when I realize that the day has transitioned into night. All the lights in the living area and kitchen are on. "Are you serious? I'm sorry."

"It's okay. You needed it. I'm just upset I woke you."

"I appreciate that you gave me this chance to sleep, but you should have woken me up earlier so you could take a nap too. In fact, why don't you have one now." I stand up and lift the blanket Beth placed on me.

"Not necessary," she says, waving me off. "I'm not tired. I slept for too long this morning." She maintains her smile while I try to clear my throat. "I'll grab you some water," Beth says as she moves toward the kitchen.

I don't get the chance to thank her before she's gone. Then it hits me: I've been asleep for seven damn hours. "Wait, has he come back or anything? I shouldn't have slept at all. Something could have happened."

"Hey, hey. Calm down, Karen. Everything is fine. He hasn't fully returned. But I did catch him driving past the house slowly every so often."

I feel my face tighten. "What? Really?"

"Yeah, it's strange." Beth hands me my drink.

"He doesn't stop?"

"Every time I saw him."

I take a gulp of much-needed water and shake my head, not knowing what to make of that. "So, he's checking up on us?" I ask trying to gauge Beth's opinion.

"Could be. Or he could be messing with our heads. It's just another piece of crazy to add to the day, I guess."

"Indeed," I say, almost at a whisper as I set down my glass. I stand on two feet and try not to fall over as the world spins for a few moments.

When I regain my balance, I take a wander over to the window and peek out the gap to see no car there. "And I take it our cells are still down? Wi-Fi too?"

"Yeah. With him driving around, keeping his distance means we're still stuck in here like two prisoners."

"I'm sorry," I say.

"Don't be. At least not yet. I've been doing some study for school next to the window while you were out. It sounds silly, but the distraction was a huge welcome. Plus, I needed to do it for my test tomorrow morning."

I stare at Beth. Is she assuming this will be over by then, that everything will have been resolved peacefully, allowing her the opportunity to get back on with her life? Not knowing what to say, I smile and hope to God she moves on to another topic. Unfortunately, we don't have many other things to discuss. Not while we're trapped.

"So, Karen, I was wondering."

I hate it when someone starts a sentence this way. The unknown fills me with more anxiety than anything else.

"You know how you had to go into witness protection after you testified against Zach?"

"Yeah," I say, feeling my body take a step back in defense.

"The thing is, and correct me if I'm wrong, but don't they give people in that situation a new identity?"

My heart races. "They do," I mumble.

"Does that mean that Karen Rainey isn't your real name?"

Beth's bombshell of a question stuns me. My mouth falls open to speak, but the words in my brain can't seem to form.

"I'm sorry to ask; it's just the thought has been driving me nuts. And I think we've bonded well during the short time we've known each other. I want to call you by the right name."

I've never been asked this before and don't understand how to respond as I grab my cell from the coffee table and check the signal. "Still jammed."

"You don't have to say anything if you're uncomfortable. Please, just forget I mentioned it. It's not important. I was just curious is all."

"You're right," I blurt. "Karen Rainey isn't my real name. It was the identity they offered me five years ago when this all began. I've had to live every day of my existence since then pretending to be another woman. They gave me some made-up history of Karen's life and expected me to forget my past and become her overnight. The initial year of it was pure hell. I had to leave behind anyone I cared about by being declared dead, only to lie to every single new person I met. And even once the heat died down and I moved out here, I still had to continue living as Karen. I can't go back from the lies, meaning I'll always be Karen as long as my ex lives."

Beth stares at me with shaky hands. "I'm so sorry; I shouldn't have—"

"No, it's fine, Beth. I'm the one who's sorry. You'd think I'd have learned to deal with my life after such a lengthy time. If you really want to know, my real name is Marie. Marie Williams."

"Marie Williams," Beth repeats. "Funny, you don't look like a Marie."

A half chuckle comes out. "I don't feel like her anymore either."

Silence fills the air in the room. I feel a weight crush me down I can't seem to shake off as I try to think of something else to talk about.

"I need to go to the bathroom," Beth says, speaking first.

Nodding to show I understand, I let out my breath. Beth walks away from the living area toward the single bathroom we share. I doubt she needs to use the toilet. She simply has to get as far away from me as possible to process everything I've told her. I get it.

When Beth strolls back out into the room, a bright light sweeps in through the thin curtains of the house, casting shadows from the metal bars that keep us safe while keeping us trapped inside our own rented space.

We both freeze and stare at one another as a vehicle pulls up and parks in the same location the man in the suit had before. Beth creeps up to the curtain and peers through to see what's happening outside.

She draws her head backward from the window and faces me with an open mouth. "It's him. He's back."

CHAPTER TWENTY-THREE

Marie

"What's made him finally stop this time?" Beth asks. "For the last seven hours, all he's done is driven by without stopping. Now he pulls up into that same damn spot just to stare straight at us through the window."

I don't have an answer. I thought with everything I experienced with Zach I'd have some clue why he would drag this all out. At any moment, he could have told his goon to attack. He could have asked him to stampede on through the house to end both my life and Beth's in a heartbeat. But here we are, still alive. Still waiting. Slowly losing ourselves with every minute that passes.

Beth moves aside from the window to pace around and mutter more to herself while I lean on the kitchen counter. I'm not hungry in the slightest. I need to be away from her. She's been like this since Zach's man came back and since she found out my real name isn't Karen Rainey but Marie Williams.

I haven't considered my true name in too long a while. It's the only way to cope with the change. It sounds strange to even think it in my head. Marie Williams. I shudder at the thought. It's like meeting a person for the first time. You shake hands and they tell you their name, but it doesn't match their face. You end up giving them the name that suits them in your mind. And from that day on, no matter how hard you try, you can't remember the name they told you.

I assumed I'd feel like a complete impostor with the name Karen, but it grew on me. Slowly, I became her to survive using a simple system: let no one into my life. No exceptions. Beth is complicating that with her kind yet curious heart. And I understand. If I were friends with someone like me, I'd demand to know everything.

"Karen?" Beth says, saying my name from close by. "I mean, Marie, sorry."

"That's okay. Takes time to get used to."

"Yeah it does. I'm making coffee. Did you want some?"

I stare her and can see the day has aged her a little around the eyes. Does it hurt her feelings calling me Marie? Is she hiding her frustration behind a mask?

"That would be amazing," I say. I need the caffeine hit to help keep me awake. Now it's nighttime again, anything could happen. Zach seems to be bold enough to make his move during the middle of the day or the night.

"It's funny," Beth says. "I thought I'd lose it not being able to see what's happening online, but I'm getting used to it, you know."

A smile streaks across my face for the briefest of moments. I had to abandon all social media when I left my old life behind. Sure, social media wasn't as popular five years ago, but I still shared a laugh with my friends and knew what was going on in their lives. Now, the best I can do is stalk them all alone—something I should give up on.

I see Beth fumbling with the milk from the fridge and step over. "Why don't you have a break. Go lie down for a bit. I've had my rest; it's time for yours."

Beth shakes her head. "No, I can't. I need to stay awake for you, Karen. Sorry, I mean..." She holds her hands over her mouth.

"It's fine. Just call me Karen if it makes things easier. My actual name is irrelevant. And best you forget it anyway. Then you have plausible deniability. You can pretend not to know my real name or my ex's. Then he can't hurt you." My words sound like lies.

Beth continues with her coffee making. She finishes up and hands me a steaming mug of the lifesaving liquid, prepared just the way I love it. This girl is too good to me.

Our drinks go down smoothly. We both place our cups into the sink by habit. I reach out and grab the two mugs to wash them up. The water spurts out, causing a horrific noise and finally ceases to flow.

"What was that?" Beth asks.

"No," I utter. I don't have to say another word to know what's happening. Still, I need to confirm the horrible thought running through my head. I charge to the bathroom and run the tap in there. Same result. The animal outside has turned off our water. What's next? The electricity? Would he throw us into the dark with no water and a limited supply of food? This has gone beyond torture.

"The water doesn't work!" Beth yells when I move back out of the bathroom. "Why would he turn the water off? Is he a lunatic?"

"Something like that. I think this is the next phase of the plan to force us outside straight into danger."

"But that's our water supply gone. We have none in the fridge."

"He's stepping up the game," I say as calmly as I can. "Something's forced him to move things along. All we—"

Without warning, the power to the house shuts off. One second, I'm staring at Beth's bewildered face; the next everything is thrown into darkness. Only the streetlights from the front of the living area provide any form of relief.

"Beth," I say to where she was standing only a moment ago. I can hear her breathing spike, so I walk slowly toward her. "Keep calm. I promise you we'll get through tonight if we stick together and—"

I bump into the back of the sofa. "Beth? Where are you? Are you okay?" The breathing has stopped. I wave my arms around to locate her nearby, but it's no use.

"Beth?" I call again. My voice cracks and loses any confidence it was commanding earlier. Has he taken her? Has he come inside to do what Zach paid him to do?

"Beth?" I whisper, closing my eyes.

I never thought I'd die like this. I never once figured I would cause the death of a life well before its time, either, but here I am, crippled in the dark, waiting for a blow to strike from the shadows.

The floor creaks around me. Footsteps. I feel the weight of another body ever so slightly force the ground to dip down and back up again with each step. A hand grabs my wrist, forcing me to flinch.

"It's okay. It's just me," Beth says.

I open my eyes to catch her standing by me in less darkness than before. Her cell's flashlight allows me to see again. "Beth? Where did you go?"

"Sorry. Didn't mean to scare you. I got turned around in the dark and ended up walking into the hallway. Then I remembered my cell."

"That's okay," I say to the outline of her face. "Just don't take off again like that."

"I won't. We should stick together and find more light before we trip over something."

"I have a large flashlight in my room. We can save the battery on your phone."

"Good idea. Let's go before—"

A force crashes hard against the front door.

"What was that?" Beth says.

I don't speak. Instead, I remain frozen, stunned by the sudden interruption.

Beth holds her cell's light up to the main entry. It fails to pierce through the darkness in any kind of meaningful way, but we can just make out the shape of the front door.

A long silence takes hold as we both fix our gaze in the same direction. What the hell made that big bang?

Beth turns as she lowers her cell. "Maybe it was a bird or something? Maybe we—"

Three huge thuds pound on the door, snapping my neck around to the source of the disturbance, along with Beth's cell.

There's no denying the sounds blaring out at us. Zach's man is at the front door, ready to let himself in.

CHAPTER TWENTY-FOUR

He's at the front door. It's finally happening. Zach has sent his last communication from prison to this maniac in a suit. I always thought Zach would prefer to be here when it all went down. I know he loved seeing the look on the face of anyone who betrayed him when he found them. But I guess a proxy is better than letting me continue to live unimpeded while he rots away in prison.

The banging at the front door stops. Beth and I wait in silence, each stuck staring at each other's faces.

"Has he left?" she asks.

Before I can answer, the sound of pounding on the door is replaced by something far worse: a cordless drill. Beth and I listen in as he begins to drill through the first deadbolt, smashing it to pieces in an instant. It's the weakest one. There are still three more deadbolts for him to destroy though, including the heavy duty lock I rarely engage. They'll slow him down, but they won't stop him coming through.

"Where do we go?" Beth asks.

I glance at her and back to the noise at the front door. It limits our options. We either barricade ourselves further into the house or we make a run for it out the side door while Zach's guy is distracted trying to break the locks. The answer is obvious.

"The side door. It's our best bet while the drill is making all that noise."

Beth nods. "Okay."

I rush at the door and unlock it as the drill is still spinning. I stop the moment it does to hear the second deadbolt clatter about and fall to pieces on the floor inside the living room. He's not wasting this opportunity and drills into the third lock. I continue working on the side door and get stuck on the final heavy-duty deadbolt that matches the one at the front of the house.

"Come on, dammit," I mutter. Why did I think it would be good to install a lock that was too stiff to be of use? Sure, it's a hard bolt to break into, but my wrists sting anytime I've had to use the damn thing.

The third deadbolt falls inside with a clatter. He's onto the last one while Beth and I are still here. We have to get this open.

Beth charges up and helps me twist the lock sideways. The key that lives inside the deadbolt feels like it might snap at any moment. If it does, we're dead.

We both grunt and groan as the key budges and turn. The lock disengages. "Yes!" I shout over the sound of the drill. I don't care if he hears me at the front, whoever he is. I grab the handle and twist as I move through what I think is an opening door, but my body slams into a wall. It's still shut. "What?"

"Isn't that all four locks?" Beth asks.

I nod. "Definitely." I know this house inside out when it comes to security. I even remember which bars on the windows are the strongest and weakest. I grab Beth by the shoulder. "Come on. Let's push on it together. Something must be blocking the way."

We both get into position to ram into the exit. I hold my fingers wrapped around the knob. "On three. One. Two. Three." We slam our shoulders into the door as I twist the handle and hold it twisted. All the while, the drill continues to make progress on the final deadbolt at the front door.

The two of us grunt and groan against the thick wood of the reinforced door I paid to have installed in the house the second I moved here. Something is blocking it from opening, and it feels like there's an elephant leaning on the side of the house to restrain us from getting through.

"Open, dammit," Beth yells. "What the heck is this?"

"He's blocked it," I say, realizing all too well a method Zach and his group used to block a person from leaving a room. He and his crew would bring along metal wedge pieces that would fit underneath the small gap in a door. He'd hammer them in so no one could open a door from the other side.

"How do you know?"

"Trust me. I know." I shake my head.

"So you're saying we're trapped then? We're stuck?"

The sound of the fourth deadbolt breaking apart pulls our attention. "Let's go," I say as I grab Beth by the arm and drag her to the corridor toward my room.

"Wait. What are we doing?" she asks.

"Not letting this asshole reach us." We charge through to the hallway as one. The front door bursts open, clattering about with more metal debris. Beth glances back and trips over the cheap runner rug in the opening, dropping her cell. It hits the ground with a crunch, turning its flashlight app off, throwing us into darkness.

CHAPTER TWENTY-FIVE

Adrenaline is a funny thing. Not only does it help us handle a fight-or-flight moment but it imprints these times in our lives onto our long-term memories almost better than any other experience. We all remember the time we faced real danger and had to choose whether we met it head on or if we ran away as fast as we could to survive. We tell those stories to every person we meet. Today will forever be in my brain. That much I know for certain.

In the dark, I pull Beth along to my room, my pupils dilating to allow enough light in as possible. We reach my bedroom and charge inside, guided by moonlight filtering in through the barred windows. I slam the door hard. "Hold the handle and press your whole body against it."

"Okay," Beth mutters. "What are you going to do?"

I don't stop moving and rush over to my cupboard. I fling it open and drop to my knees to find what I'm looking for.

"Oh my God!" Beth yells. "He's pushing on the door."

"Don't let him in. I've almost found what I need."

"Hurry," she whispers.

The door bulges. I don't know how she's stopping him from barging through. I can only guess fear is giving her the strength to fight and survive.

"Got them," I say as I pull out two door jams from a dusty box. I rush back and install them as fast as I can where Beth is standing. The second I'm done, she falls to the ground exhausted. She sits there, catching her breath, while I check on the locks again. I bought the door jams ages ago, planning on placing the reinforced devices on the front and side doors. But I soon realized they would be too inconvenient to use regularly. I figured the extra thick external doors and barred windows seemed enough to keep unwanted guests out. I was wrong.

"That was lucky," Beth says in a hushed voice.

"Yeah, I don't know about it being lucky. More paranoia saving the day than anything else."

Beth chuckles. "Whatever those things are, they've just saved us."

"For now," I mutter. I look up and hear the man in the suit banging on the door with his fist. "Dammit," he yells through the wood as he stops. The next thing we sense are his footsteps as he walks away, back to the front door to swing it shut. I figure he doesn't want to be interrupted by anyone walking by to see the entrance to the home has been drilled open. It's only a matter of time before he uses another tool to cut through this internal door in front of us. I never thought I'd have to pay for a special barricade within the home itself. If only I had taken that extra step and built a panic room.

Needing to know where our invader is at all times, I press my ear against the door and listen. His footsteps seem erratic and unfocused. Have things not gone down as planned? Were we not supposed to retreat further back into the house? I soon realize he must be on the phone as I pick up his muffled voice. Is he speaking to Zach? I'd kill to give him a piece of my mind.

"Can you hear what he's saying?" Beth asks.

I shake my head and press my ear tighter against the door. He's still chatting, but I can't understand a word. Frustration takes over. "How is he using his cell?" I ask Beth. "He did the same thing outside near the garden shed."

She shrugs in the dull light. "I guess he must have a way to get only his phone to work through the jammer." Beth steps back from the door. She seems to be coming down a little from the excitement, only allowing herself to think about where we are now. It's a lot to take on, I know. I'm doing what I can to stay ahead of complete and utter defeat. The second I give up is the exact moment Zach wins.

"What now?" Beth asks.

I pull my head away from the door and face her. What do I say? I've got no other moves left to use. We are trapped inside my small bedroom with no way to communicate with the outside world while some crazed man tries to smash his way inside. I realize the truth.

"We're done. All that's between us and that guy out there is this door. The second he breaks through it we're dead."

"No. You can't be serious," Beth says as her breathing intensifies. "There must be something we can do. You must have an idea or a plan."

I don't say a word. I can't think straight. Instead I move to my bed and sit down. I hoped we'd find a way in here. My idea was to run in and jam up the door. We managed to pull that off. Beyond surviving for another moment, I had nothing else up my sleeve.

"There has to be something we can do," Beth whispers.

I pity her optimism. I prayed we'd come out of this thing alive, but Zach planned this well. How could I beat him? He's spent years thinking about this while I've sat around wasting the same time hiding away from the world in a giant rut.

"Karen," Beth snaps, grabbing my attention. "Sorry, I know that's not your name, but we can't just close down and give up. Not now."

"Why not?" I ask.

"Because," Beth says. Her eyes dance around my room, seeking a solution. She won't find one. "Because, it's not over. He's not bashing on that door yet. Something is holding him back."

I can't imagine what. He seemed determined when he was using a power drill to break his way inside the house. But he keeps talking on his cell, pacing around the living area. Maybe we still have a chance to escape.

I turn to one of the two barred windows in my room and smile.

CHAPTER TWENTY-SIX

I'm not sure if it was panic or defeat making me forget about the windows in the house, but every one of them can have their bars removed. It's just a matter of unscrewing the frame that wraps around the glass.

I fish through my cupboards again, hoping to locate a screwdriver. I know the tool has to be in here. Hell, at this stage I'd accept something left over from an Ikea box.

"Anything?" Beth asks.

I shake my head without answering. There's annoyance in her voice. I told her my idea a moment ago and was a little surprised to see her not jump up and down for joy. She voiced her concerns about trying to remove the bars when we should work on a 'better' idea. I had none, and she wasn't pitching anything. So for now, this was the plan.

It had gone quiet out in the living room. I don't know what to make of the absence of the man's voice. He isn't trashing the place by the sounds of things, so I have no clue why we are still alive.

I reach the end of another carton and retrieve a small pocketknife. I'm about to toss it back in its box but think better. Not only can I use the thing to defend myself, but it might just serve the purpose I need more than anything else.

"Please work," I mutter as I stand and move toward a window. Beth steps out of my way.

"What's that?" she asks.

"A pocketknife. I'm gonna try it on the window bar screws and hope for the best."

Beth crosses her arms over her chest. It's not cold in the house at all, so I can only imagine that this is a comfort thing.

I pull the blade out from its protective casing. It's not a full Swiss army knife that comes complete with a screwdriver, but it will have to do. I stand on my bed to get closer to one window. I press the point of the knife inside the grooves and attempt to twist. Nothing budges.

"Please work," I say. "Don't let this be it. Not now." I keep trying the blade at different angles and pressures, but it's no use. Nothing wants to turn. I struggle to think about how old these bars are and if I've ever maintained them. I installed them within the first week of living here. I never once sprayed the ends with lubricant oil. All I ever thought to do was to check how secure they felt.

"The window's too old, isn't it," Beth says.

I try to ignore her question as best I can until the tip of the blade snaps, sending my hand through to punch one bar. The pain is instant. "I guess so," I reply with a gasp as I pull my arm back a moment to shake it out.

"Taking the bars off would have been too easy," Beth says.

I let a sigh escape my lips as I fold the knife back in and throw it on my bed. It bounces off onto the floor. "What else will go wrong?" I yell before I slump down on the mattress and press myself into the wall, defeated again.

Beth doesn't answer my hypothetical question and moves back to the door. She takes a quick listen in for our aggressive attacker. She doesn't flinch or move. Why isn't he on the other side of the door ripping it apart with his bare hands?

I glance up to the bars above, knowing freedom is beyond the small barrier. The pain in my hand burns my knuckles but it's nothing compared to the agony in my stomach as I realize how damned we are.

"Maybe he doesn't want us dead. Maybe he needs us contained."

My head lowers to Beth. "What are you saying?"

"Think about it. Why hasn't he drilled his way through yet? It's only a cheap internal door made of wood and cardboard, right? You may have blocked it with those jams, but one swift kick would snap it in two."

I screw up my brows at Beth. "So what does that mean then?" She shrugs. "Maybe your ex wants you alive."

"Why would he want me alive?" I ask as I turn away from her.

Beth stares at me. "That's the million-dollar question, isn't it? You won't even tell me what he did to make you testify against him. Like I said before, tell me everything about your life—the good and the bad—and I might be able to help you shed light on this messed-up situation like no one has before."

My eyes dance around the limited space of my scarcely decorated bedroom. I've kept it bare and dull this way for a long time. I never wanted this place to feel like home.

"I know you think you're protecting me by keeping me out of the loop," Beth says, "but I'm telling you we're beyond that point. Whoever that guy is out there, I'm on his list now too."

A sigh comes out of me thick and fast. "So I'm just supposed to tell you everything about my screwed-up life, am I? What good does that even serve? You'll think less of me than you already do."

"No, I won't. We are trapped inside this house because of your ex. He's had complete control over this entire ordeal from the first minute. If he wanted you dead, you'd be dead. Simple as that."

"He's torturing me before he gives the order for that man to squeeze the trigger. I know it."

"But why has this man outside waited so long to do something? I don't mean to be so bleak, but it just seems like it wouldn't be that hard for a hired killer to get the job done. Maybe this guy has been told not to harm us."

I shrug. "Maybe. It does kind of feel like we've been deliberately scared into a corner. Or maybe this guy isn't a professional because Zach couldn't afford the kind of killer who'd get things done with more discretion."

"Maybe," Beth says. And I don't think she believes me.

I close my eyes and place my head back against the wall. I can't take much more of this hell. Why can't Zach just end it all now?

Beth sits down on the edge of my bed. "Let me in. Let me know the real you. Maybe I can make sense of what he is doing and put a stop to this."

I open my eyes and focus on Beth. Her words sound illogical but also, they don't. I'm close to considering what she's asking of me until I see the knife on the floor. I scoop it up in my hands and pull out the broken blade. It's still sharp. Enough to cut skin.

"What are you doing?" she asks as I pull myself away from the wall and head to the locked door.

I glance back over my shoulder. "Putting an end to this."

CHAPTER TWENTY-SEVEN

A lot happens in a split second. We can make a decision, one that might alter our life in such a dramatic way that we never recover from it again. We all face these moments in our lifetimes whether or not we want to. It could be our own stupidity bringing us to the total chaos that is human existence or something beyond our control. Ultimately, it doesn't matter. Because deep down, I believe we are the masters of our fate, which sadly means one thing: our mistakes are no one else's but our own.

The first doorjamb comes off easily through a sheer delay in Beth's reaction time. She grabs hold of me by the shoulders before I get my hands on the other one, not giving me the courtesy of a free second.

I feel the floor come up beneath me harder than expected, causing me to roll on my side. My head slams into the mattress, but I maintain my grip on the broken knife.

"What the hell are you doing?" she asks me as she fixes the doorjamb. "He could have heard that."

"Good," I say. "I want him to know I'm coming for him. If he thinks he can burst into my house with a power drill and intimidate me, he will have to earn it."

"Have you lost your mind? You're talking about fighting a man hired by Zach. You put him away for life, remember?"

I don't answer.

"Well? You put him away, didn't you?" Beth asks again.

"You know I did," I spit out, doing little to contain my anger.

"Then you understand better than anyone that what you were about to do was suicide."

"Maybe. Maybe not," I sneer. I hear my own words, but they don't sound like they're coming from me.

Beth crosses her arms over her chest. "It was. I may not have the full story, but I've heard enough to understand you were about to go down with a fight."

I jump to my feet and shove the knife into my back pocket. "You don't know me!" I yell.

We both hold our firm gaze on one another, each breathing louder than is necessary. I hate yelling at Beth, but she's leaving me little choice. I can't stand anyone assuming they know who I am, that they can sum me up within a few moments, because I'm not just the weak coward they all see before them. They don't know what I've been through.

"Okay, maybe I don't know the real you, but you need to stop hiding behind that fake name of yours. Let someone in for a change. Let me help you, for God's sake."

I hold back on going right off at her for shoving me to the floor and realize she wants to learn everything about my past. Is it curiosity driving her forward, or genuine compassion? "Why?" I ask. "I don't deserve to be helped. I told you to leave when this all began with a clear warning. You should have listened."

Beth doesn't flinch. She doesn't even blink as she holds her gaze on mine. "What happened? What made you turn against your ex and send him away forever?"

The memory hits me in the gut like a bullet and keeps drilling. It rips through my veins and tears my skin apart like a fireball until it reaches my eyes and throws acid into each retina. The strength breaks from my bones as I fall into a heap and cry. I can't hold back another moment as I see two eyes condemn me to a life of suffering. Even if I wanted to tell Beth what happened, my mind won't allow me to speak.

She grips my shoulders again, but this time they don't grasp on tight to throw me aside. Beth wraps her arms around me. "Shh. It's okay," she says.

I try to push her away, but I fail to stop the comfort she provides. It's clear I need this. I've needed it for so long, but I don't deserve happiness or the right to feel human again, do I?

"It's okay," Beth says again.

If only she knew the truth.

CHAPTER TWENTY-EIGHT

I don't know how much time passes with me in Beth's arms. It's most likely a few minutes ticking by in reality, but hours pass by in my fragile mind. Either way, I feel my body letting go of all the tension I've been carrying for the last five years.

"Open the door!" a male voice yells. Three loud bangs follow his demand.

I squeeze my eyes shut tighter than they already are, trying to will the man away, but it does nothing to stop him yelling.

"I'm coming in," he says.

The attack is timed to perfection. He waited until Beth and I were at our most vulnerable to break down the weak barrier that exists between us. Can Zach see inside my room? Did he choose this moment to send in his goon, or did my stupidity screw me over one last time?

The cracking of the wood and cardboard splinters through any calm Beth had generated within me. We fly apart and rise to face the demon at our door. I lay wide eyes upon the pissed-off man in a suit who looks ready to rip us into little pieces.

Beth scampers away to the wall as he rushes in. I attempt to hold firm but feel a weakness overpower me. All I can do is watch while Beth charges at him and tries with all her might to defend the bedroom from this creep who has spent the last day watching us. She stops the second he produces a pistol from the small of his back and aims it square at her head.

"Don't move."

Beth doesn't. She holds her palms up while her lungs play catch up. "Please don't shoot," she whispers.

He doesn't reply to Beth's request and instead shifts target to me. "Hands up."

The reality of the situation finds me, forcing my body to comply. I raise my sweaty hands.

"Turn around, both of you."

We each shuffle a one-eighty to face the opposite direction. Is he moving to hit us over the head? Is he going to shoot while we turn our backs? I get my answer sooner than expected.

"Place both of your hands down behind your backs."

I do as I'm told and feel a single gloved hand grab my wrists and pin them tight together. He has more strength in that one limb than I do in my arms and legs combined. The weakness takes over once again.

A second hand places a plastic zip tie over both of my wrists. From experience, I know that's what it is being employed to restrain me. Zach showed me how he used to secure key personnel inside the banks he robbed.

I realize that the man has placed his weapon away to secure my hands. If I communicate the fact to Beth, would she attack him again? I don't want her risking her life just for me though.

The moment passes once he moves onto Beth and secures her wrists tight the same way.

"What do you want from us?" she asks.

"You'll know soon enough," he says. "Now turn around and move out into the living room to the sofa. It's too squashed in here."

"For what?" Beth gets out, saying the words my mouth and tongue seem to be incapable of doing.

We are turned and shoved through the door. I feel the splinters of wood under my shoes crunching with each stride. The darkened hallway feels hard to navigate when bound like this, causing me to sway in my step and collide with a nearby wall.

"Stop screwing around," he says, prodding the gun into my spine. The weapon is back out and in play. I'm lucky Beth stopped me from charging at him with that broken knife. The damn thing almost got me killed.

The man's pistol fails to right my path, sending a strong arm out to grab my shoulder. He guides me through the hallway along with Beth and out into the living room. A quick shove sends me toward the sofa.

Beth and I settle next to each other as best we can, considering our hands are tied behind our backs. She doesn't take her eye off the man while I attempt to avoid his gaze.

"Don't move," he says as he paces to the front door. He opens the broken entry and digs himself into the electrical box that is fixed to the portico wall. I hate it being there all exposed the way it is. It's no wonder he was able to throw us into darkness so easily when all I can do is put a padlock on its flimsy door.

He activates the power to the house once again and the lights flicker into life. He comes back inside, closing the door behind him. "Much better," he says, taking a stool from the kitchen bench that is supposed to be a breakfast bar. Papers fall to the ground and scatter. Neither of us has ever used the seats for more than a place to stack junk.

He slides the stool across the floor. The man takes a seat and holds his firearm out, keeping us both still. I take in his image, trying my hardest to recall what he looks like should we survive this ordeal. He's just as Emilio described. Our attacker has cold blue eyes, thick brows, and a thin five o'clock shadow. He also has long brown hair that flows down to his neck. He is wearing a black suit with a light blue shirt and dark blue tie that all seems out of place on a good day, but I'm no expert.

"So," he says, shifting his attention between us. "Here we are."

"What do you want?" Beth asks, acting as the more confident spokesperson.

"Oh, you'll see," he says. "I promise."

CHAPTER TWENTY-NINE

I feel myself shutting down with every moment that passes while I stare ahead at the long-haired man with the gun. I don't know what else to call him. He sits on the tall kitchen stool and keeps a firm grip on his weapon.

"Time to make a phone call," he says.

"How?" I ask. "You jammed the signal to the house."

A smile comes from his lips. "And what, you thought I wouldn't have a way to work around it?"

I get the sense he doesn't enjoy being asked questions, so I go silent, not liking the response he gave me.

"What about you?" he asks Beth. "Got any questions for me?"

"No," she says with a lowered head.

"Didn't think so. Now, let's get down to business. It's going to be a long night otherwise." He removes himself from the stool and approaches us both. We shy away, each hoping not to be the center of his attention for any longer than we have to. Using the barrel of the pistol, he gently raises my chin up to his eye level.

"This has all been about you, just so we're on the same page," he says.

I don't argue with him. I know why we are here, with each person in the position they're supposed to be in.

"Funny to think how you could induce so much trouble." The gun moves aside from my chin and over my face as he brushes some of my hair out of my eyes. The cold metal scrapes against my skin.

"I'm not trying to cause anyone any problems, I swear it. And I'm sorry if I have."

The man laughs. "Bit late for that, sweetheart."

I know it is.

He stands tall again and steps away from me for a moment. "Now, as I was saying, this has all been about you from the second you received that gift yesterday. That's the way you like it to be though, isn't it. You may act otherwise, but I think you want all the attention focused on little old you and your pitiful existence."

"No. It's not like that. Why would I want any attention on me? I live in a house like this so I can escape the world I left behind."

"Is that so?" he says with a sneer.

"Yes."

Keeping his eyes locked on mine, he moves over toward Beth. She lifts her head to see him coming and reels herself in and away from his approaching form. It does nothing to stop him.

"Shh, Beth, it's okay. Say, tell me, do you trust your housemate?"

"What?

"It's a simple question. Yes or no?"

"Why do you—?"

"Answer the damn question!" he yells, drawing closer.

"Yes," Beth says.

The man stands with a smirk. "That's good to know," he says as he returns the gun to the small of his back. "Guess it's time to make that call then."

Beth and I both look at each other. I see the confusion covering her eyes. She doesn't realize what will happen next. I understand all too well who the phone call will be to and why.

"I'll be back in a minute," he says with his cell placed against his cheek and his index finger raised to show he needs quiet.

The second he turns away, I whisper to Beth. "Are you okay?"

"I'm fine. Who's he calling?"

I turn, squint at our captor. "Zach."

Beth doesn't reply. Instead we try to listen in on the private conversation happening in front of us, but it seems impossible to make sense of a single word.

"Why?" Beth asks.

I face her. "Why what?"

"Why is he calling your ex?"

My head drops, fighting against an invisible force. "To hear his next set of instructions, I suppose. This thing will only get worse before it gets better."

Beth wriggles in her chair, leaning closer. Her face shifts like the wind. "What did you do? What happened to cause all of this?"

CHAPTER THIRTY

The conversation in front of me seems to be lasting longer than it should. But then again, conversations about your fate will always take longer in your mind than anything else. I try to focus on that and ignore Beth's question.

"Well?" Beth says. "Something crazy must have happened, right? You said so yourself that you are the reason Zach is serving a life sentence in prison. Tell me what he did to trigger such a reaction from you."

I lean over wishing I could squeeze the bridge of my nose tight. I don't want to look this somewhat naive girl in the eyes when I think about the past. "It's beyond complicated, Beth. Why do you need to know so badly?"

"Because, Marie, or whatever name you like to be called, we are about to meet our end if we don't find a way out of this. Tell me what happened. Maybe I can think of something to use to our advantage."

"I don't see how this could work."

"It's easy. I'll think of what to say to buy us some time. Right now, I've got nothing to gain this clown's attention. I'm simply collateral. Please, give me anything to work with here."

My pupils swap between Beth and the man. "Okay. I'll try to force it out before he comes back. This won't be easy."

Her eyes light up a little. She needs this to keep her sanity levels afloat. I'm the reason we're in this mess. If I can brighten her life with my secrets before the end, so be it. I owe her that much at least. I hope she doesn't spit in my face when I get all of my story out.

"It started about six years ago when I met Zach. I was a bartender, of all things, in an upscale bistro in Long Beach, California."

We both check on our captor and see he is still busy. Beth nods for me to continue.

"During a shift, Zach came in and chatted me up. This was the first time we'd met, but he was so confident, I swear that he already knew me from somewhere else. We get to talking about a few things until I mention to him about the worst experience of my life I'd had the week before. I was at the nearby bank putting in my paycheck when three masked men came charging in the place armed with pistols and shotguns. Within minutes, the trio cleaned out the tills, took anything of value from the bank's customers and got the manager to open the main vault. They left moments later with a huge sum of money. From the grin on his face alone, I could see he was one of the three. He'd caught sight of me during the robbery and figured in his arrogance he'd track me down to hit on me. The bastard used the ID he'd stolen off me from my purse to find me."

"What did you do?" Beth asks.

"He intrigued me. Here was this young idiot around the same age as me who looked like a local surfer telling me he'd robbed the bank I was just in. I guess his claim impressed me despite my understanding of how pathetic the whole thing was."

"It happens," Beth says. "We've all wanted the bad boy from time to time."

"But I knew better. At least I should have. Fast forward a year and I'd been seeing this moron on and off while he continued to rob a bank every so often. I understood it was wrong for me to be with a man like that, but there was something about him that was different to the rest of the people in my life. He was the exact opposite person who everyone wanted me to associate myself with. Not to mention how passionate he could be when we were alone."

Beth holds her attention on me, not bothering to look at the man in the room with the gun who is still on his cell.

"Things between us took a turn when I discovered he'd been seeing another girl my age casually. We were never exclusive or anything like that, but it still hurt when I realized I wasn't enough for him. I should have told him earlier that I wanted to take matters seriously."

"Is that why you turned him in to the police?"

"No. I wasn't that petty. I was, however, stupid beyond belief. I thought I needed to impress him. I figured if I could show him I was the better option, he'd love me and only me."

Beth remains quiet. I can tell she doesn't want to interrupt. Instead her mouth stays open. I've left her gobsmacked with my nonsense. I realize I shouldn't be saying what I am about to say to her, but I have to. It needs to come out. I have buried it within for too long, allowing the truth to rot me from the inside out.

"What did you do?" Beth asks.

The memories flood in, washing over any strength I have left. Piece by piece, I'm falling apart. "We were driving along, late at night. I'd known for about a week he'd been spending time with another girl. I could smell her on him whenever we met up. I didn't dare reveal what I knew though. I thought I could fix things and make him love me, but I only made everything worse."

"It's okay," Beth says. "Just let it out. What did you do to fix things?"

I force myself to continue. "We stopped at a gas station to grab something to eat. We didn't need fuel. Before we left the car, I snatched a mask he kept in the glovebox and put it on. I told him I would rob the place. He thought I was joking until I grabbed his pistol too.

I rushed out and charged toward the store, knowing there wasn't a second mask or gun for him to use. I'd be doing this on my own and showing him how wild I was. He'd have to pick me over anyone else. How could he choose another lover over me? Me, the one who ruined everything the second I flew into that gas station like a lunatic."

A lump forms in my throat as tears sting my eyes. I try to speak. I try to fight through the pain coming through each word that spills from my mouth, but it's too much to handle.

"What happened next?" Beth asks.

"I... I can't..."

"Hold it together," Beth whispers. "Please."

But I can't. I shake my head and try to shy away from her.

"Come on. You can do this," she says.

The man returns from his conversation before I regain my ability to think straight. I lower my eyes to the point where I only see his legs and the end of his gun swinging freely in his arm.

He grabs my chin with his spare hand and forces me to look him in the eyes.

"Enough chat. It's time to step things up a notch."

CHAPTER THIRTY-ONE

I stare ahead at the sight before me, unsure whether I'm in a dream. The long-haired man has put his pistol away only to replace the lethality of the tool with an oversize hunting knife. It's the kind that looks sharp enough to split a hair in two, and he's waving it around and at me while he rants and raves. I'm still trying to recover from my memories.

His words blur into the background. I can't hear him. I feel aware that I am blocking him out while he makes threat after threat against me. Little does he know how much I despise myself.

He moves the knife to within a few inches of my throat. "Do you want to die like this? Tied up while sitting on this crappy furniture in this run-down house? Well? Do you?"

I shrug, just to give him an answer.

"This isn't a joke. I've been sent here for one specific reason, so I would take what I say seriously."

I let my eyes fall away from his. Something I can tell he hates. "Do what you have to," I reply.

"Oh, I will, don't worry. There's no chance in hell you'll get out of this. But first, you will confess."

"Confess?" I ask, glancing up to him. "What are you talking about?"

He grins wide at me, happy to have my full attention. "You need to come clean about what you did and tell me on this phone the real reason you've been hiding away from the world for five years." He pulls out the cell he was using a moment before and hits a button to record me via video. His hands place the device down on the coffee table. He leans the cell sideways against a stack of coasters with the lens angled up toward me.

My eyes flick between Beth's, the phone, and the man. Confusion consumes me. "Is this what Zach wants? Why?"

"You know why," the man says pointing at the phone. The reason I'm not dead is because Zach wants me to tell the world on camera what I did. He wants everyone to become infuriated with the deal the authorities gave me that put me into witness protection while Zach got sent away for life. Killing me would be too simple. He wishes me to suffer.

"I won't do it. You'll just have to kill me." I turn from him. I'd cross my arms if I could to show my defiance.

"Is that so?" The man moves aside from me for a moment and paces in a small circle. He's grappling with something in his mind, struggling to make a heavy decision no doubt regarding me.

I lean back on the sofa and close my eyes. How much longer do I have until he lashes out and strikes?

"I guess you'll need a little persuasion to talk," he says with a low voice.

I sit up straight to see the man grab Beth around the neck as he brings the blade up to her throat. "How about now, huh? Have I got your attention?"

"Please don't hurt her," I say as I swing my entire body to him. "She shouldn't be here. Just let her go."

"Not a chance. Not until you admit the truth."

My own throat closes up as I see the knife press against Beth's. Blood draws slightly from her youthful skin. How can he do this?

"Tell me!" the man yells.

My lip quivers. Tears flow down my cheeks, clouding my vision. "Please, don't—"

"I said, tell me," he repeats as his muscles flex and tense up, ready to end a young girl's life in one swift movement.

"Okay!" I scream. "I'll talk. I'll confess everything. Just don't hurt her, please."

The knife eases away from Beth but stays close by. The man points at the cell phone and nods for me to express my story into the camera.

I take a deep breath and focus on the device as he leans over to adjust the angle slightly. I let out a lengthy sigh before beginning my story. "My name is Marie Williams, and I... well, I accidentally shot a young boy named Tommy Price five years ago in a gas station near Long Beach, California. After the accident, the kid got placed in an induced coma in hospital and was kept alive via a life-support machine."

I squeeze my eyes shut but my tears can't be stopped. A dam made of concrete and steel couldn't prevent the flow of pain that is surging through my soul in this moment. I am dead inside.

"Continue," the man says.

I open my raw eyes and feel the air fall out of my lungs. I take a few seconds and glance up to Beth. She won't so much as look in my direction. Despite having a knife near her throat, she'd rather ignore the threat on her life to avoid eye contact with me.

"I went in to rob the gas station to impress my boyfriend Zachary Sanchez. The store was empty, not a single customer stood inside. I held up the station's attendant without a fuss. He was distracted on his cell until he saw me in a mask pointing Zach's gun at him. The till got emptied fast. I could tell it wasn't this guy's first night being robbed, so I sent him to the back room away from any hidden panic buttons near the register."

"It was all going to plan, I take it," the man says.

"You could say that. I didn't plan this thing in the slightest. It was a spur-of-the-moment decision I can't believe I ever undertook. Things went okay to begin with, then it all fell to pieces. I was on my way out, grabbing a few items for the road, when the attendant came running out with a shotgun. I spotted him at the last second and ducked down behind the end of an aisle. He fired at me anyway and sprayed the store. His own stock went flying everywhere. Apparently he'd had enough of being robbed. I was the straw that broke the camel's back. Still, I returned fire to send him backward into the rear room so I could get the hell out of there, but he wouldn't stop. He kept moving at me, one shell after the other until he'd reloaded a few more into the gun. I had no choice but to crawl to the other side of the store to escape."

I take a moment to close my eyes and breathe, knowing what's coming next. The man allows me this brief window to compose myself.

"I sent a few more rounds toward the attendant as he did the same to me until I ran out of aisles. I could see he would come around the next corner and run me down with another volley of shots, so I figured it was time to stop his attack before he killed me. Everything seemed to slow down. I dropped to the edge of the aisle as he approached and fired my last bullet. But it wasn't the attendant standing there. It was a young boy, no older than five or six. I shot him in the chest and... I didn't mean to. I never saw him. He was just a scared little child trying to escape the store. He got caught up in a gun fight between two stupid adults who should have known better."

I feel the air drain from my lungs, forcing me to take in large gulps to recover. I throw both hands over my mouth and do what I can to stop a panic attack from crushing me. After a few decent breaths in, I refocus. I have to finish.

"I froze on the spot as my pistol fell to the ground. My legs didn't run to the kid to see if he was okay. Instead, I sat on my knees, powerless to move. Zach came in a second later and got me. He dragged me away before I could find the courage to help that little boy. We fled the scene before the police or an ambulance could arrive. I found out later that the kid's name was Tommy Price and that they placed him into a coma after doctors operated on his small body to save his life."

Beth can't stop moving her head left and right as if she is searching for a way to escape the room. I can tell she hates to be breathing the same air as me. I don't blame her.

"The police caught up with us within a day and arrested me for attempted robbery and attempted murder. There was no way they'd let me get off easy. I was set to go to prison for a long damn time, but at the last second a federal agent came in and offered me a deal. One I couldn't resist. One I didn't deserve, but it saved me nonetheless while sending Zach away for life."

My head hangs low as the weight of my confession drags me down. I don't feel good admitting the truth. There's no cathartic breakthrough cleansing my soul. Instead, the worst part of my history has resurfaced. I'm a monster.

The man's strong hand grabs me by the chin to lift my face up as he squats down. He wants me to look him in the eyes when he kills me. I realize he has let go of Beth entirely and that she is standing behind him. It seems he's finished using her to get to me. I try to make eye contact with the scared young woman but fail to catch her focus. Now that she knows the truth, she won't ever speak to me again.

I look to the man and see the knife inch closer. "Please," I say, "just get it over with. I deserve to die."

The knife presses up into my neck. This is the end.

CHAPTER THIRTY-TWO

The tension mounts in the man's muscles as he pulls back harder on my hair. The knife at my throat presses deeper and deeper against my skin. Through what little air I can muster, I provoke him to do what he came here to do.

"Go on, kill me. You know you want to."

"Not yet. Not until I've broken you. Not until you've suffered."

A thickness ties a knot in my stomach as I swallow his threat.

"Now that I have your confession, it's time to share these words with the world."

"What do you mean?" I blurt.

"We'll see what society has to say about someone who shoots a child and runs away like a coward."

Is he saying what I think he's saying? Is he going to spread the video online?

The knife slackens, letting me breathe again. As I regain control over my lungs, I stare at him in wonderment, certain I understand his intentions. If I'm right, my world is about to come crashing down harder than it already has.

The man doesn't speak as he paces circles around me. I don't know what else to call this demon who won't spare me from shame as he moves in close to place a solid grip on my shoulder.

I want this all to be over. There's no way in hell I'll watch my confession play out online. I can imagine the comments poorly typed out by judgmental strangers, the endless stream of op-eds blasted on the web, fueling the mob to take over and demand blood. "Please don't," I beg.

"Shut up!" he yells. He releases his grip on me and shoves my body to the ground. I lay sideways on the disgusting carpet and stare up to the coffee table, my hands bound behind my back. I can just see the cell phone he used to record everything sitting on the glass surface. Instead of killing me and putting me out of my misery, Zach has paid this man to put me through some personal hell first with the video the device captured. I can't let that happen. I won't.

My lungs go into overdrive as my eyes dart around the room. The air comes and goes from my chest in short uncontrolled blasts. The walls close in as the floor presses hard against my face.

"Get up," he says as he kicks me in the ribs, pushing the air out of my lungs.

A shudder escapes me as he grabs my wrists at the small of my back and lifts me up with no effort. I feel so weak in his arms.

"Now you'll sit here and watch as I upload that little video we created to YouTube, Facebook, Instagram, Reddit, and any other social media platform that comes to mind."

"Please... don't," is all I can mutter.

The man smiles as he glances at Beth. "Do it."

"Do what?" she asks, stunned.

"You're going to put this file online for me," he says, jabbing the knife in her direction.

She stares at him without saying a word. Her inaction is an answer he doesn't seem to appreciate.

"Do what he says, Beth," I call out without looking at her. I can't have him harming Beth again as much as I don't want my worst nightmare coming to light.

"Okay," she replies. With a few shuffles, she moves over to the coffee table and grabs the device.

All I can manage is to watch as she taps out the necessary commands to upload the video to the world. I shake my head and hear myself beg.

"Please, no. Don't do this," I plead with him. "You can do anything to me. Just don't put my confession online for the world to see. Please."

Beth sets the cell down on the coffee table. The tiny device has the ability to bring my life down to its lowest level—something

I never thought possible. Her eyes dance between mine and the man's. "It's ready," she says with a shaky voice. "You just have to tap this button." She points at the screen.

The man reaches down to the phone and picks it up from the stack of coasters that were being used to prop it upright. This is it. He holds the power to share my dark past with the world in his palm. I have to stop him. This can't happen.

He turns to Beth. "Why don't you press the button and—"

I charge at his extended arm holding the cheap cell and drive my body into his mid-section until I sense the phone falling out of his grip.

"What the hell?" the man bellows, adding confusion to the room. I drop to my knees as the cell bounces off my chest and falls to the floor. Before I know it, I roll to the ground and onto my back to feel the device slide into my zip-tied grasp. Not having a second to spare, I spin the rest of the way over to my knees and push up into a run.

I don't let the yelling voice behind slow me down as I charge for the only target I have in mind, the idea coming to me as I go. Beth stumbles sideways and falls over in the trails behind as the man charges through and after me. He doesn't know where I'm going in this tiny house.

"Stop!" he yells. His hands reach out to the cell in my grip, so I clench it tighter, closing both fists over it as much as possible until I find the bathroom and do a quick one-eighty spin toward the toilet. I fall to the floor and land on the bowl, releasing the phone behind me into the water in an instant.

"No!" the man shouts. "What the hell have you done?" He tries to thrust me to the side, but I stand up on two throbbing legs and block his path as best I can while my arms are still bound behind my back. It works until he grips me by the shoulders and pulls me out of the way, only to shove me to the floor with rage.

"You stupid bitch!" he yells as I see him dig his hands into the toilet bowl with a splash to retrieve the cell. It slips from his grasp through his wet gloves and falls back in a second time. "Dammit."

I lie on my side, staring up at him while he retrieves the device again and pads it dry with his shirt, but we both know it's too late. The cheap burner he used won't be waterproof like a lot of the newer flagship phones out there. As he attempts to save the device from beads of water that are working their way inside and over the cell's chipboard, he stares at me with more intensity than before.

"You'd better pray that footage is still on there, Marie. Else I can guarantee you're in for a world of hurt."

CHAPTER THIRTY-THREE

I attempt to catch my breath in the living room. The man placed me down on the sofa and bound my ankles with another zip tie. He pulled it as tight as he could across my skin as a scowl dug its way into his face. With focus in his eyes, he watches over me while attempting to save the cell I dumped into the toilet. Beth sits beside me.

"The screen's getting worse," he growls out loud. "It's not accepting my input at all. I can't upload the damn video."

Apparently, the phone lost all capability to work when water flooded the components inside. The damage is giving me hope that the moisture will destroy the footage of my confession. There's no way in hell I'll ever say those words again in front of a camera. I'd rather die.

It still boggles my mind that I even said them in the first place. I always assumed I'd take what I did to the grave with me and tell no one who didn't already know. I guess I never thought a day like this would come.

The man places the cell down on the kitchen bench on one of my towels before he stomps over toward me. His eyes stay locked onto mine without direct eye contact. He regards me the way a farmer checks over his cattle before having them shipped off for slaughter. What thoughts are running through his mind?

He lets out a sigh. "So what should I do with you if I can't get your confession off that cell, huh?"

"Just let me go. I don't know who you are. I won't run to the police."

He crosses his arms tight over his chest. "Do you think I'm a complete moron? You realize what has to happen now, don't you."

"Yes," I mutter. I was in a mask at that gas station. And I went into hiding via witness protection the second I testified against Zach. How much effort had Zach gone through to send this psycho after me?

The man shifts his eyes up to Beth, turning himself to her level while keeping his arms crossed. "You're going to help me get a new confession."

"No, she isn't," I say trying to put any defiance I can into my voice. "Leave her out of this. Let her go." It hits me that I'm playing right into his hand. All he needs to do is threaten Beth again and I'll confess. I know it.

He ignores my demands with a smirk and continues speaking with Beth. "You understand what's at stake here?"

Beth bares her teeth. "You know I do."

I shift my focus to her. I can tell she doesn't want to do a thing in my favor after hearing my confession. She almost answers him as if I'm not in the room. It hurts, I'll admit, but I don't have a leg to stand on. I might as well be the devil to her now.

But as I hold my gaze on her eyes, I find anger and fear fighting over one another. I also spot something in there that tells me she might not completely hate me, that deep down, somewhere inside, she could see me as a fellow human being. That slither of light may be my only hope to escape this hell.

"But first, I've got a job for you," the man says addressing Beth. He points toward the kitchen. "Go put that cell into some rice. I saw some in the cupboard. While it dries out, we're going to work on a new confession from Marie." He smiles at me and chuckles under his breath.

This sick bastard looks like he will enjoy torturing the truth out of me. Luckily, I still have an item in my possession he has bothered to notice. I found it when I fell to the floor in my bedroom. It's the one element that could pull me out of this mess.

Sitting in my back pocket is the half-broken knife I had planned to stab this asshole with. Could this half-shattered piece of steel save me? Maybe. But having the object is one matter. Using it is another.

I shake my head at myself, frustrated that Zach has sent this man into my home and forced me into this situation. Why should I have to choose whether I take a risk and attack another human being with a half-broken blade? Did Zach want this day to drag out hoping it could throw me into such a dilemma? I wouldn't put it past his cruelty.

I stare at the man in the suit and realize I might have no choice but to use my knife before the night is over.

CHAPTER THIRTY-FOUR

What was I thinking? What was running through my stupid mind when I dumped that crappy cell into the toilet? My confession was done. Over with. The hardest words I'll ever have to speak out loud were no longer sitting in my core, weighing me down.

For five years, I walked around with a weight on my shoulders that only seemed to grow heavier with time. Instead of accepting what was to come next, I screwed everything up. Now the man will force it out of me one more time. I can't go through that again.

The knife stirs in my pocket. Its tiny blade is no match for the giant piece of metal sheathed at his side, but I only need it to complete a quick task to stop any questioning short.

I glance at him setting up a new cell to record my second confession. He came prepared, I'll give him that. He places it in the same position again on the coffee table. But if he thinks I will confess the way I had before, he's got another thing coming.

The last moment we spoke, I was vulnerable. I thought I was confessing to save Beth's life. Is he really moving to use that tactic on me a second time? Surely I can convince myself he would never harm her, that it was all a bluff to get what he needed? I don't know what I'll do when push comes to shove.

The man settles on a seat in front of me from the tiny dining set that belongs to the house, placing it backward the way he had before. Beth is in the kitchen, trying to save the damaged cell while avoiding my gaze at all costs.

He leans forward and crosses his arms over the top of the chair. His leering smile breaks out again, along with his knife.

"Let's have a chat, shall we? Just for a minute before I hit record." The blade rises to my face and turns sideways. He runs the sharp side down my cheek, showing me how he could cut my skin without a stroke of effort. It travels past my neck and down the front of my chest, settling near my stomach. What's he going to do?

"Lean forward," he says.

I take a shaky breath and do as I'm asked. He wraps both arms around my waist and cuts me free from the zip tie behind my back. He shifts my hands forward without placing another restraint on me. The plastic binding my legs remains.

With little concern, he raises my chin between his thumb and index finger, drawing my attention to his face to show me who's in control. "It's not looking good is it?" he says, jutting his head toward the kitchen. He's referring to the water-damaged cell Beth is attempting to fix. She's pulled the device apart to separate the battery from the body. Does she wish to recover the phone to spare me from confessing again? Or does she want it to work so he can upload its footage for the online world to digest and spit out again? Does she still care about me on some level? She has to.

I feel the man's grip force me around to his eye line. "What do you think this is, huh? She won't save you from punishment. Who would save a person who shoots a child?" he spits. "Nothing can change what you did, so why don't you make this easier on all of us and confess."

I stare up at him, feeling the raw energy of the man as if he is a priest about to dunk my head in a lake. But some sins can't be washed away with a few words and a breathless moment under water. I will never be clean again, so there's no point even trying.

He scoffs. "Staying silent now are we? That's not going to spare you this time. I can tell you now. Don't think for a minute I'm not serious."

I hold his stare. It's what he wants from me. Once he fades back, he turns and places his large knife down on the coffee table and he hits record on the new phone as if he is preparing for a friendly chat between two people. What the camera can't see is my bound legs or the dangerous weapon off screen.

"Please state your name," he says like we're in court.

My eyes shift to the cell. "Karen Rainey," I say.

He bares his teeth with a chuckle. "Now, now. We both know that isn't your real name, is it?"

"I'm not sure what you mean, sorry," I say with a shrug. I keep my focus on him, waiting to see that moment when his upper lip twitches on one side. It only happens when things don't go his way, so I've seen it happen a lot already.

"Okay then," he says. "Tell me what you know about Marie Williams."

I shake my head with a scoff. "Are you serious?"

"Amuse me," he says, both hands spreading out wide.

The confidence fades from my face. I glance around to spot Beth standing in the open door frame of the kitchen, struggling away with her wrists still bound, as she stares at me in bitter disappointment. I get the sense if it wasn't for her, I would be feeling this man's true wrath.

I turn my head toward him and see the tightening of his fists. He's a big guy whose physical strength can't be matched, but I have an idea that will render all his power null in one sweeping motion. Why is it only coming to me now?

"Well, Karen?" he says. "What do you know about Marie?"

"She..." I blurt out, unsure what to say. "She..."

"What?" he presses.

"I don't want to do this," I say placing my hands on my head.

"What's the problem?" he asks. "I thought you said your name was Karen."

"It is."

"You won't mind me asking you a few questions about Marie then, will you?"

"I guess not," I force out. "Ask away."

The man gives me a false smile as he leans back. A shiver runs down my spine. Why do I feel as if he's gained the upper hand?

"How old is Marie?"

"Thirty-five."

He nods. "Thirty-five, huh? That's an interesting age for most. It's that time in your life when you've got things worked out to a point where you know what the next twenty years will be like. Does that sound right to you, Karen?"

My head lowers with a grin to cover up the overwhelming desire I have to lash out at him. He knows that's not me. He understands I've put my existence on hold and frozen it in time. All the while, the rest of the world passes me by.

"My thirty-five was a little different from the average person's. I'd already settled down, gotten married, and had a kid. In fact, my wife was about to give birth to our second one by then."

I try to keep my face from showing any reaction to his story despite me wanting to question it more than anything else in the world. Why would Zach's guy tell me about his life? He continues.

"You think you've seen it all by thirty-five. You assume you'll know what to expect, but I can tell you now I wasn't prepared for the birth of either of my children when they came flying into our lives." He smiles at me again. This time without a hidden trace of malice. Is the memory of his kids being born helping his harsh mood? What does this mean?

"I remember the unique ways they each learned to crawl, walk, and talk. Despite being a few years apart, they both did their own thing and worked it out the way they wanted to. Fun times, I tell you."

I didn't know what to say or do. Was this a test because I shot a child? Or did he feel like talking about his kids?

"From my understanding, Marie doesn't have children. She hasn't settled down or let a special someone into her life, has she, Karen?" His eyes lower with a sneer as they penetrate any defensive layer I can use. It all becomes clear.

"I doubt Marie could ever understand what it would be like to raise a child or have a significant other, because you see she wasn't aiming to settle down by thirty-five the way most of us inevitably do. She was out there playing around in a deadly world she didn't belong in. She was out there disrupting the natural order of things."

My eyes dance through the room as I lean away from him. The more he says, the closer he gets. "I—"

"What's your name?" he asks cutting me off.

"I already told you," I say as tears spill down my cheeks. "It's Karen Rainey."

"Bullshit," he spits. The blast of his breath almost knocks me back.

"Karen Rainey is the pathetic loser you created to hide your real self. You thought you had perfected the art of blending into the background of society. You thought Karen could keep Marie's sins hidden away forever, didn't you?"

"No, I didn't!" I yell. "I know what I did. I know who I am."

He heaves his breath in and out through clenched teeth. His knuckles turn white as his grip tightens on the sides of the chair in front of him. He stands up and flings it behind him.

"What's your name?" he yells.

I close my eyes, flinching. Is he planning to hit me or stab me with the knife? All just to get me to admit what we all know to be the truth. All the while, I am wondering what Beth is doing. Is she watching? Will she help me? Or will she allow this beast to destroy me?

"I'll only ask this one more time: what's your name?"

I stare up into his eyes and sense an unwavering hate beaming through them. He wants to grab that knife from the coffee table and plunge it deep into my heart. But not while Beth is around. There's something between them. I have to use this while I still can.

"My name is Karen Rainey," I say.

CHAPTER THIRTY-FIVE

Zach's guy hits pause on the recording before he storms off to another room in my house with the cell in hand. I've never seen a man's knuckles turn so white. He's so furious he has to make Beth place a fresh zip tie on my wrists, possibly out of a fear of what he'd do if his fingers touched my skin.

I wasn't trying to get him so mad that he killed me. I wanted to discover where his line sat for murdering me while Beth was a witness to the crime.

I'm beginning to understand the influence her presence has over his every decision. I need any advantage I can find to stop the truth coming out again. When he threatened to kill Beth the first time I confessed, I couldn't tell if he was bluffing his violence. Now I'm convinced he might have been misleading me the entire time.

If I'm right, it means Zach hasn't paid this man to murder me after all but merely to extract a confession. Of course, my ex would want me to suffer in the most undignified way possible. Death is much easier to handle than having the world know the truth.

As hard as it is pushing a man close to breaking point while he wields a large hunting knife near your throat, I remind my brain the consequences of the Internet learning my dark secrets. I don't want to be remembered as the evil woman who accidentally shot a child, even if that's what I deserve. I'm not that person.

"Wow," Beth says as she steps toward me from the kitchen. We're alone and could make a run for it at any time, but fear holds us in place. She grabs the interrogation chair the man was using from the floor and places it upright a comfortable distance from me.

Before she wanders back to the kitchen, I grab her attention. "I'm sorry you've had to hear these things about me."

An audible sigh erupts from Beth's mouth. She shakes her head at me and takes a seat with bound arms. "I don't want to hear any excuses or justifications. We simply need to escape this situation and that's all. As soon as we're safe, I'm leaving."

I understand and can't argue against her decision. My eyes fall to the floor. "I don't know why I pushed him like I did before. I guess I do but it's so stupid. I should admit the truth and get this all over with."

Beth doesn't blink. Either she's had enough of me, or she doesn't want to become involved. I'm on my own.

From where I sit, I may only have one bold move left to play if Zach's man pushes me to my limit for a second time and it won't be easy. Still, I can't let the truth escape my lips again.

Beth smiles at me. It's not a happy face I'm seeing, but an expression laced in sarcasm. "I look forward to your next performance." She pushes herself up and walks to the kitchen, toward the broken cell phone.

"Why are you so desperate to fix that thing?" I ask. "Are you just trying to save your own ass, or do you want me to pay for what I did?"

She stops, placing the back of her head to me. "Do you think I enjoy being here knowing what I know?" She turns around and faces me again, not looking me in the eye as she leans against the kitchen doorframe.

"I—"

"No," she says, cutting me off, "I don't. I hate to be studying this far from home, in this city, in this crap hole of a house with someone as disgusting as you. But here I am."

I shake my skull as tears threaten to drown my eyes. I wipe them clear before anything can develop. My head falls forward with the weight of Beth's words. I try to speak but nothing comes out. She fills the silence between us.

"This man though, that's another story. He clearly wants you to pay for all of this. I don't think he'll be happy until you admit to what you did on camera so he can show the entire world the truth."

I lift my head up to her eye line. "Why does the whole world have to know? Don't you think I've suffered enough already? You've seen this life I live. You've experienced three months of it. Imagine five years."

She doesn't change the look on her face and keeps her arms crossed. "Maybe you figure you've paid for your crimes, that this is all a big waste of time in the grand scheme of things, but Zach certainly isn't satisfied yet. And I doubt he'll stop anytime soon."

"No matter the cost to me?" I ask.

Beth chuckles.

"What does that mean?" I almost yell, forgetting that the man could hear this.

She holds up both of her palms to hush me a little. "Consider this, Marie: this guy is trying to extract a confession out of you while I'm still here as a witness. How long do you think he'll keep doing things that way before he finally snaps? You realize I'm all that stands between him and you."

"I know," I mutter. "I've known for a while. It just sounds more real coming from your mouth."

"I'm sure it does. So maybe it's time you talked before tonight turns ugly."

My eyes dart about the living area. I thought I had a way out of this mess that was foolproof, but I realize it won't work. In the dull lighting of the living area, I notice none of the house's imperfections lining the walls and floors. All I see is the front door and the various holes drilled into it. I have to get out of here before it's too late, before Zach's man loses control.

CHAPTER THIRTY-SIX

The man has returned from his backroom break to the living room. I avoid eye contact with him the second he enters the limited space. He already despises me as it is. No one in this room needs another reason to hate me.

Beth's words still rattle around my head. He's losing control. Soon he won't hold back, and his true fury will break out to tear me to pieces whether Zach has paid him well enough or not. Maybe the time spent to find me only added to the hatred my ex felt.

No amount of pleading can make his attack dog understand that I didn't mean to shoot that little boy and cause such a rip in Zach's world. I never pictured myself testifying against him to help put him away for life, but it happened. This man though seems to take my past harder than some hired gun, making me guess he could be related to Zach. Hell, he could be a fellow criminal who's recently gotten out, keen to get vengeance for his brother-in-crime for all I know.

What am I supposed to think after a day like this one? All I do recognize is there's too much hard evidence stacked up against me for Zach to ignore.

Zach's man doesn't head for me and instead walks straight to the kitchen, past Beth, to the fridge. Before I know it, he's got the door open. A few beers find their way into his hands. They belong to Beth as I never touched the stuff.

With cans of liquid courage in his firm grip, he heads over to me and places the drinks down on the coffee table with a thud. He grabs one beer with his oversize paw and cracks it open. A moment later, the can is tossed back so the man can take a huge slurp. Some beer spills down his neck to his now-crumpled suit as he gulps down what looks like a third of the beverage.

The can slams down on the table, spilling a few drops onto the glass surface. A wafting of foul breath floats in my direction. I don't know if this is part of the man's new tactic to torture me or if he wants a beer to get himself through whatever it is he has planned. A quick glance to Beth doesn't give me any answers.

"Still think she's on your side, huh?" he says with a grin as he pushes back his long messy hair and opens his jacket. "Don't make me laugh."

Has he noticed the doubt in her eyes? Has he heard the contempt she holds for me within her voice? He must.

I stare into his eyes and ignore his comments about Beth for a moment. What happens when my confession reaches the web and I've witnessed the aftermath in full? Will he then receive fresh orders from Zach to follow through and kill me? Would Beth be disposed of as well due to everything she's seen and heard?

I can only assume he's planning on killing me the second my new confession has spread far enough online. Otherwise, the rage flowing from his soul doesn't make much sense. The second cell comes out again, already recording.

"So, you don't care to admit who you are," he says, continuing our conversation from before. "That doesn't matter. The Internet will see you on the recording alongside a clear and recent photo of your face. I'm afraid changing your name won't help you avoid the past this time, Marie. That's not the way the world works."

I hold his gaze. "Is it? People escape justice for what they've done every day. Tell me something: how long did it take Zach to find me? How long was he actively looking?"

The man stands over me and grabs my shoulders. "Every damn second after you got Zach sent away for life despite shooting an innocent child." He chuckles to himself. "The world's a pretty screwed up place, huh?"

I shake my head ever so slightly. "And who are you in all of this? Why do you care so much about me getting what I deserve?"

The man stares straight through me, penetrating my soul with his eyes alone. "All you need to know is that I'm where I should be. It's just a shame finding you took so long. I could have been here sooner."

His answer tells me he is more than a hired goon for Zach. If only I could figure out the extent of their relationship. "Was it worth the hassle?" I ask.

The man chuckles. "It will be. Especially if we can save that little video we made. Then you can watch it spread like wildfire online. Everyone will get to see you for who you really are, Marie."

"It was an accident," I blurt. "I never meant to shoot that kid. I would never want such a thing to happen, but it did, okay?"

"Oh, is that right?" he says, leaning closer than before. "This holier than thou attitude didn't stop you from taking the deal though, did it? You've never been upset for what you did to that child. You only cared about what it did to your life."

"That's not true," I say.

The man releases his grasp on my shoulders and stands all the way up. He grabs his beer again and takes another huge swig. Most of the liquid empties into his mouth before he wipes the excess away with his sleeve. That, combined with the sweat pouring off his back, is ruining his suit.

"You think you've got it all worked out," he says, "I'm supposed to feel sorry for you, am I? Guess again, Marie. I didn't come all this way to discuss your interpretation of the past five years. I came here for a confession, and I don't care what it takes for me to get one."

CHAPTER THIRTY-SEVEN

"I'm never going to confess," I say out loud to the man's threat. I regret the words the second they fall out of my mouth, but I had to say them.

"Oh, you will," he snaps. He takes out the knife again and stabs it down hard between my limbs. I flinch and close my eyes, convinced he's just plunged the weapon straight into my thigh. I open an eye and squint to see the blade sticking in the couch and not my body.

"Next one won't miss," he whispers into my ear.

My arms and legs shake as I generate enough courage to say what I plan on saying to rattle the man's cage the only way I can figure to. "You and I both know that knife is for show. If you wanted to use it, I'd be cut up and bleeding already."

He pulls the blade out of the sofa and chuckles at me. Beth receives his attention for half a second as if he is checking for her reaction, eager to keep her full of fear. He no doubt can't afford to lose the edge he has over us both. "You assume you've got this puzzle solved, don't you. I can't harm you while the confession is still up for grabs, can I. Or better yet, you assume I won't make you suffer with a witness watching over us. That's it, isn't it."

His question throws me. I can't answer him without giving away what I know. I try not to reveal anything with my face, but from the grin he gives me I recognize it's already too late.

"Maybe I should send Beth here away and lock her up in her room. It's not like she could escape through those bars you have on the windows. Then we can really get started on things here. What do you think?"

"You don't have to do that," I say, sounding pathetic.

"No, it's a brilliant idea. She doesn't need to see this, does she? After all, it's your fault she's here. You're liable for any harm that befalls her."

"No. I tried to warn her. She wouldn't listen."

"Enough!" he yells. He glances back to Beth as if to dismiss her from this situation. "Why don't you head to your bedroom and give Marie and I some time to talk alone."

Beth glances at me and back to Zach's man. With a nod, she complies and walks toward her bedroom. My mouth falls open as I watch her leave without a fuss. The door to her room shuts a moment later, sealing my fate.

"There we go. Alone at last," he says as he plays with the knife. "Now, where were we?" He pretends to think out loud. "Oh, that's right."

Our eyes meet. "Please, you don't have to do this. Whatever your connection is to Zach, I guarantee you hurting me won't make things better."

He chuckles again. "There you go, thinking you can bargain your way out of this. But you know what? Maybe giving you pain is what's needed to bring balance back to this situation we find ourselves in. We spend so much time trying to convince each other we can talk matters out, that violence isn't the answer. What happened to the simpler times when life wasn't so damn complicated, huh?"

I close my eyes, unsure if he's serious or messing with me. I have to think of something, of anything to say to bring Beth back out here before he does what her presence has stopped him from doing.

"Open your eyes," he says. "You don't get to look elsewhere. You can't just run off like you did in that gas station and leave a young boy for dead. There's no deal waiting for you to sign to make this all disappear." He presses the weapon down against the top right-hand side of my chest.

"This is where you shot him, isn't it," he says, trying to hold my gaze. "Do you think Zach would have ever fired his weapon at a kid? He wouldn't, right? Yet here you are, free as a bird."

I feel the blade press in and pierce my skin through multiple layers. Blood seeps out my clothing as I do what I can to fight against the pain. I can't let him win. The blade twists a little in the small wound for what feels like an eternity.

Finally, the knife lets up. I gasp for air.

"Look how strong you are. Not a single flinch. I'll bet that really hurts too."

"Not at all," I say through gritted teeth.

"Is that right? Maybe we should make this interesting then, seeing as you're so tough." He pulls out his pistol from the back of his pants and jams it into the fresh wound.

I scream, unable to fight through the pain this time, and wait for him to squeeze the trigger. He presses the gun as hard as he can into my chest.

"Screw the confession. Tell me why I shouldn't put a bullet in you right now and end this."

I shake my head, but no words come out to back up my failing argument. I can't speak through the searing pain in my rib cage as it sends lightning bolts down through my entire system.

"Dad!" Beth yells out from the hallway.

"Dad?" I whisper in a fog. Did Beth just say what I think she said or am I dreaming?

The man yanks the pistol out of my chest. He looks up to his daughter. I twist around as best I can to see her from this side of the sofa.

"What?" he asks, hands out wide.

"This isn't what we agreed to. And besides, do you think she'll confess again if she's dead?"

My brain spins inside my head. What's happening? Who are these people? I stare at Beth as she walks further into the room and settles beside her father. I try to speak.

"Confused, Marie? Allow me to introduce myself," Beth's dad says as he cuts his daughter's restraints away. "My name is Steven Price, and this is not Beth. This is my daughter, Toni Price."

My eyes almost burst out of my head and dash between the pair. Their surname—Price—It can't be. "Wait."

Beth leans down and sneers in my face. Everything about her demeanor changes in the space of a few seconds. The horrible thing I did wasn't to a complete stranger. She's related to Tommy Price. They both are.

Her hand leaps out and grabs me by the throat. She moves to within an inch of my eyes. "You shot my brother," she whispers, "and the whole world will know about it."

CHAPTER THIRTY-EIGHT

Toni Price – Five years earlier

Tommy's coma had gone on for a month. I couldn't stand seeing my baby brother like that. In the past, he was constantly on the move, always charging around the place, exploring the world. Tommy had been that way from the moment he could crawl.

I remember when I was still at home, midway through my senior stages of high school, when he'd rush around on all fours from one end of the house to the other, only concerned with the journey. He never seemed to worry where we were or what we were up to. He'd just crawl along the floor, soaking in life through his oversized blue eyes.

It went without saying that Tommy wasn't a planned child. I was sixteen when he came into our lives. I didn't like the idea of having a baby brother to handle while I finished up high school as I'd gone this long without one. I was supposed to be concentrating on getting through the next few years so I could get accepted into a college of my choice. Instead, I would have to contend with a crying kid at all hours of the night.

My mother went from being an attentive rock, on which I could always depend, to a sleepless wreck who didn't have the time to deal with my 'teenage crap' as she so lightly put it. My father became a walking husk, always out working overtime as an EMT to keep the money flowing in. Things had changed.

Needless to say, I was your typical teenager at that age. I thought the world was against me, and I couldn't see past my own needs to the bigger picture. At least not until Tommy first smiled at me and grabbed hold of my pinky finger with his entire fist. I never thought you could go from feeling indifferent about a living thing to loving them so unconditionally that you'd do anything to defend them.

Despite the difficult time we were having as a household, we all realized the presence of Tommy enriched our lives. I'd always wanted a little brother or sister to boss around when I was younger, but my parents feared bringing another child into the world, as I too was an unplanned baby. My mom and dad had never aspired to be a mother and father, but I came along either way. It seemed Tommy resulted from history repeating itself. It was just a shame he couldn't have been born ten to fifteen years earlier.

Nevertheless, we were a family, and I wouldn't have traded places with anyone. Having such a young brother matured me quicker than I realized. Suddenly, there was someone else to put over my own needs. And nothing could compete with watching the little guy learn and grow.

The sound of the multiple monitors beeping away brought me back from the past, reminding me we were in a hospital sitting around Tommy's broken body. The machines kept him alive. My mother sat closest to him, always holding one of his hands in hers while my dad stood against the wall, arms crossed. Anger coated his face to the stage where I didn't remember him having any other expression. I knew deep down it killed him to sit there and see his little boy that way while he remained powerless to do a thing about it.

The silence between us was deafening. I felt like opening the closed door to allow the sounds of the ward staff to flow in. I didn't know how to deal with the situation. There I was, about to turn twenty-one with a six-year-old brother in hospital on life support.

Not being able to stand another second of the nightmare, I got up out of my chair and moved to the single window that held a demoralizing industrial view. It was ugly, but it was better than the sight of my broken family.

I thought about what my dad had told me, about my baby brother being shot by some criminal in a gas station in Long Beach, California. Tommy was in the wrong place at the worst possible time, caught between a moron struggling to rob the store and the store attendant working to defend his business. They fired at each other in the open with no concern about who else might be around until the robber 'accidentally' shot Tommy.

The bullet struck my brother high in the right-hand side of his chest. The piece of lead actually bounced off his bone and struck him in the skull so hard his brain swelled.

I couldn't stomach the thought someone would do that to a little boy whether they meant it or not. And, to make matters worse, it was all my fault. My dad, my mom and my brother were all coming up to visit me on campus in Los Angeles. I was studying to become a registered nurse, motivated somewhat by my father being an EMT. They had accepted me into a course that was over a thousand miles from home.

During a short break, my family flew over from where we lived in Lakewood, Colorado just outside of Denver to surprise me. I flew home during the breaks, but this term I couldn't afford it. I'd spent the extra money I earned from the two part-time jobs I had on clothing I didn't need. My mom and dad knew I would be homesick and missing them all, so they made the effort to come to me.

Having never stepped foot in the Los Angeles area, they turned the trip into a worthwhile one by seeing the sites before they came to visit me. They toured Hollywood, Beverly Hills, Santa Monica, and spent a few hours down at Long Beach soaking up the sun before the surprise. It was on the way back up in their rental car that things took a turn.

My father was filling the sedan up with fuel while Mom slept in the passenger seat. Tommy should have been doing the same after the lengthy day they'd all had, but he was wide awake and hungry, according to my dad. Wandering into the store on his own, Tommy did not understand he would end up in the middle of a shootout between two insane people.

It's my fault he was there. If I'd only been able to restrain myself from wasting my money, I could have afforded a plane ticket to fly home. I could have prevented my family from coming up. Then Tommy would have never been shot by some desperate robber and placed on life-support, fighting for his young existence.

CHAPTER THIRTY-NINE

Marie – Now

My mind is spinning. The family of the boy I accidentally shot has discovered me, tricking me into assuming it was Zach who was out to throw down a line of revenge upon my very existence. I don't know which is worse: me thinking Zach had sent someone out to kill me, or that Tommy Price's kin has found me.

I'm staring at that little boy's father and sister, absorbing their hatred, still trying to comprehend that Beth isn't who she told me she was. I took her in, believing she was just another student looking for a room to rent. She seemed so innocent from the moment I met her. Whatever she did to fabricate this personality is beyond impressive.

The Beth I know is gone. The gentle caring college girl who stayed when I warned her to leave was all but a fake. In her place is Toni Price, the older sister of the little boy I never meant to hurt. The thought makes me think about the brother she told me was a cop. Was that nothing but a lie? Without a doubt. She misled me for three months pretending to be a sweet, dedicated student. What else was just words from her mouth designed to make me believe she was Beth?

Toni stands back from me in the living room as if the air I breathe is toxic. She sees me staring at her for too long and steps forward with a newfound confidence I hadn't seen in the version of herself she once showed me.

"I'll bet you're freaking out, huh?"

I nod, not knowing where to begin. I still feel like I'm talking to Beth, but I'm not. The whole time 'Beth' and I were trying to escape the man hanging around in the street, she was pretending to be on my side, playing me with ease. All just to get a confession.

Every setback we had, each strange thing that happened, Toni was the one behind it while communicating with her father. Every time she left the room or when I didn't have eyes on her, she must have been on the phone with her dad somehow. Or maybe they'd bugged the house, giving him the ability to listen in on our every vocalized thought. I feel a sickness wash over me.

"Look at her," Steven says. "Like a deer in headlights."

I ignore his insult and think more about Toni's lies as Beth. The Ethernet cable wasn't broken; she destroyed it. Insider knowledge of my paranoid security setup allowed her to work my cameras, window bars, and deadbolts against me. She and her father also knew all about Zach and my relationship with him. They adopted our past as much as possible to drive me insane. The Latin note was the ultimate cherry on top that sold it all. They could have only gotten that perfect detail from Zach. Did they visit him in prison?

Toni steps closer, stopping in front of my feet with a smirk. I wince at the pain in my chest and shoulder and stretch my neck. Locking eyes, I say the only words on my mind. "Who are you?"

A chuckle escapes the contempt on her lips. "You don't get it, do you?"

I feel my heart skip a beat as her father joins in on her laughter. I'm the only one in the room who doesn't comprehend the joke. A fatal mistake.

"But don't worry, you'll face the true me before the night is over, Marie. And who knows, maybe we'll even meet the real you."

I try to respond to her threat, but nothing comes out but choked words. What does she mean? In my attempt to stay sane, I think about our fake names. It sounds odd not hearing Toni call me Karen. But it's just as crazy she isn't a Beth.

Our pseudonyms no longer matter. Everything has changed. The only truth I recognize is that the person I thought was a friend who may have seen through my faults, hates me beyond what seems possible. I've never felt such loathing burn within a person's eyes. I can't blame her though. How can I? If our roles were reversed, I'd feel the same way.

The father and daughter move away from me and discuss what to do next in private. Steven's still holding his knife. It's been bloodied by my body. I wonder how far he would have gone if Toni hadn't have stepped in when she did?

They're after my confession to replace the recorded one that may no longer exist on the damaged cell phone sitting in rice in the kitchen. I can only hope the footage is destroyed, because that damn phone captured it all.

The cheap cell got every screwed-up word of pain I caused that boy along with his family. The recording made it clear the reason I escaped justice for what I did, and they want the world to experience and share their anger first hand.

"Why did you come out here?" Steven asks Toni like I'm not in the room. "I had things under control. She didn't know who you were or about us being related to Tommy. We've lost that edge if we ever want her to confess again."

She doesn't answer straight away and gives me a sideways glance instead. "I know I blew our cover, but I could see you were losing control."

"I wasn't."

"Dad, come on," she says, hand on hip. "Don't lie to me. We both appreciate the temptation is there, but we have to work through it together and get her to confess. If we kill her, the truth will die by her side, and she'll avoid being punished for what she did to us."

Toni's words jab into my soul like a hot poker straight out of a fireplace. She talks about my life as if I'm disposable. But her carefree words make me think. Have I avoided anything for all these years the way she thinks I have? I've spent half a decade in mental agony, running away from who I thought was the biggest threat to my existence. The realization of the Price family, and not Zach, trying to find me this entire time hits hard.

All I can wonder is what took them so long.

CHAPTER FORTY

How did the Prices find me? Dustin comes to mind. Did he notice that these people were after me at any point? He barely ever mentioned them over the past five years. After the authorities released me from custody, he told me I'd never see the boy's family, that I was better off knowing as little about them as possible. I can say one thing without a doubt: either he didn't know what they were capable of all these years, or he was lying.

My brain takes me to Toni. She lived in my home for three months as Beth before this moment. Who in their right mind could do so with a person who had shot their little brother? And why did she wait so long to make a move? Either she didn't have the guts to ask me the right questions, or she never knew if I was the right person. After all, I wore a mask into the gas station.

She couldn't have known I shot him at first. Her behavior was consistent right until she left to go see her parents for a week. It wouldn't surprise me if she had found out who I was in that time. It justifies her odd actions and thoughts during our fake ordeal. Several times she tried to steer the conversation into territory I wasn't comfortable with no matter my reaction. She asked me questions that were far too personal in her attempt to extract the past from me.

The discussion in front continues and I can see where it's heading. My time is fast running out if I wish to survive tonight and escape. Not that I deserve to. I should push them further and further until they go over the line. But I won't do that. Despite all the anguish and self-hatred that's clouded my brain over the last few years, I still prefer to be alive. I want a second chance. I only told Steven otherwise because I thought he would kill Beth. Now I don't know what he or his daughter have planned.

Champagne Beach flutters through my mind, calling me. Will I ever see that place? I doubt it. I'll never feel its pure sand between my toes or smell the spray of unspoiled ocean water as it wraps itself around my body. Karma won't let me escape this. Paradise is just a dream now.

I think back to that moment when I realized I had shot the young boy. The gun fell free from my hand and clattered over the hard floor of the gas station. The wild attendant saw what I had done and stopped firing upon me. He too dropped his weapon. We both froze, unsure what to do. The next thing I knew, Zach was whisking me away.

All I remember from that point was him shouting at me as he sped off from the scene. I tried to convince myself I hadn't just shot a little kid in the chest. I couldn't have. What kind a person would do that and leave? Plus, I'd barely used Zach's pistol before, only having fired at bottles that were lined up along a fence out in the desert while being half drunk with him. I couldn't hit such a small target.

But I did.

When the attendant came charging out, I fired back to defend myself. I should have surrendered right there and then and thrown my gun to the ground, but I wanted to prove something to Zach so he would see me as the crazy, fun girl to keep around, and not a forgettable mess. I demanded to be his number one, but my pathetic desire got a boy hurt.

The dad, or Steven Price as I now recognize him, moves closer and stares down at my frail body. He's such a tall guy who I now know is capable of anything. His eyes are wild, and his nostrils are constantly flared. With good reason.

He wants to harm me and make me suffer. I shot his kid. Put the little man in a coma. If I were in Steven's shoes, I'd have the same thoughts plowing through my head. Maybe worse.

I don't know what happened to his boy despite checking the death notices like a maniac before and after my arrest. I did so for years. Now, I only look every so often, running the name Tommy Price through all the databases I can access at once. Nothing ever came up. Had he awoken from the coma and identified me? No, I had that stupid mask on. Which means I can only ask myself something I've been trying to avoid since Steven and Toni both told me who they are: would they even be here if Tommy was okay?

"Dad?" Toni says, her voice urgent. He swivels to her and nods, communicating on a level I have no way to interpret.

Steven turns and takes another step forward. If he is about to do what I think he would love doing, I have to ask the single question that's flooding my mind.

"Is he alive?"

Steven's eyes narrow in as he stops. He stares at me without blinking. "No."

My shoulder's drop. Tommy is dead. At some point, his parents had to pull the plug, so to speak. The innocent kid I shot died. I murdered him. Tears roll down my cheeks again. This time I'm not concerned for myself. How can I be?

"Do it," I say.

Steven doesn't move an inch. He stares.

"Do it. I killed him. I shot your boy right in the chest. He's dead because of me. You know I deserve this."

The knife comes out again. It's not long before the cool metal is pressed against my throat as Steven grabs my hair and shoves my neck back. With my wrists restrained behind me, I can't stop him. "Go on," I say through the pain.

I close my eyes and wait for death to release me from this life. I'll never see Champagne Beach or escape the lonely existence I once lived, but no longer will I have to live in a constant state of fear.

Once this is done, I can be free.

CHAPTER FORTY-ONE

Toni – Then

I t'd been six months. Six long months of visits back and forth to the hospital to see my brother still in his induced coma. I moved home and put my nursing studies on hold. The last thing I wanted to think about was college when my little bro remained trapped inside a hellhole. Mom and Dad begged me not to, but I asked them why my life got to continue on while someone froze his in time? They didn't give me an answer, so I suspended my course load.

I had to be there for Tommy despite not wanting to spend another second in the hospital halls. I couldn't stand the smell of cleaning agents working overtime to fight off the disgusting odors and germs only a ward could produce. How many gallons of chemicals did they have to splash over the floors of the building each day to keep it clean? It was thoughts like that my brain focused on toward the end.

For the first three months, insurance covered everything. Then the company called and told us they could no longer fund Tommy's coma, that we'd exhausted all options and would need to finance his medical care from our own pocket. So that's what we did.

We all pitched in. Dad continued to bust his ass as an EMT while Mom took up a part-time job to help pay for Tommy's round-the-clock care. I got a position at a local coffee shop and offered every dollar toward the hospital. When we weren't working or sorting things out at home, we were in Tommy's room, each of us tired in our own way.

Dad and Mom communicated less and less as the days dragged on. It was as if they could no longer stand to be in the same space as each other. I even once tried to start a conversation they'd both have to be a part of to no avail. All they offered me were one-word answers or grunts like a pair of teenagers.

Despite all efforts to earn money, my parents had to dip into their savings to keep Tommy going, but after three months of funding, it was all in vain. The doctors gave the news as best they could. Tommy's diminishing brain activity meant he would never come out of the coma they'd put him in. In the first few months, he was still in there, fighting against the gunshot wound to his chest that had ricocheted into his head, but the battle took a change for the worse.

Slowly, over the last few months especially, his EEG showed a gradual descent. We held on ourselves, ever hopeful that things would turn around. We each believed he would somehow push back and fight his way out of oblivion. He had to; otherwise, what was this all for?

I visited him as much as I could. We all did at different times. I'd read to him and tell him what had been happening in the world while I played his favorite music as loudly as the hospital staff would let me. But it was all a painful waste of time.

After six months of being placed into the coma, Tommy's brain activity reached zero. He was gone. All we had left was his half-machine body. I could almost see the difference when I looked at him. Something was missing. No longer was my baby brother lying before me but a withered husk.

My parents gave the doctors permission to turn off his life support. It was the right thing to do no matter how much it hurt us all. Tommy's frame didn't last long either. In less than two days, they pronounced him dead, but we all knew that he had died six months ago when that piece of crap robber shot him in the chest.

I stowed my anger away in time for Tommy's funeral. I had to be there for my struggling parents and doing so full of rage would not help one bit. There's nothing worse than watching a child get buried.

I'll never forget his tombstone:
Thomas Price
Son of Steven and Laura Price
Brother of Antoinette Price.
2008 - 2014

It was the last line of his tombstone that hurt the most. Seeing such a short date range was devastating. It seemed like a blip in time you'd see on a resume and not a representation of a person's life. I couldn't help but think about the things he'd miss out on, the experiences he would never know. Who would he have met and bonded with if he'd been given the opportunity to grow up?

Almost two hundred people came to pay their respects. They were all from his life. Classmates and parents, aunties and uncles, grandmothers and grandfathers. The most surreal moment was seeing Tommy's great grandmother attending. There she was in her nineties, shuffling along, closer to death than anyone else in the room to see off her daughter's daughter's son. It was backward.

I cried so much at the funeral I ran out of tears. My eyes instead burned away in their sockets leaving behind red streaks of pain. When my time came to speak, I froze up on the stage and stared out at the sea of faces all locked onto mine and felt my jaw clench. I charged off without a word and hid in the church's rear.

Mom saved me by taking my place despite having stated that she couldn't handle the task. I listened in a back room while my dad comforted me as best he could. That was the worst part of it all. No one could make me feel better, no matter what they said or did. I was a useless waste of space that needed her little brother. But nothing could bring Tommy back.

When the funeral was over, I went home with Mom and Dad, sitting on my side of the car the way I always did. Tommy's spot was empty. No booster seat, no collection of toys strewn about the floor, no sign he was ever there. I burst into tears again, worse than I had the entire day. I couldn't handle seeing that vacant sight. Is that what happened when we died? Did we vanish into thin air as if we'd never existed in the first place?

When we got home, no one knew what to do next. Driving to the hospital had given the three of us hope and purpose. Having a reason to get out of bed every morning when all you wanted to do was hide under the covers kept the remainder of our family going.

Now Tommy was dead and buried in the ground at the local cemetery. There was nothing left to do but to find a new reason to get up in the morning and move on with our lives.

Easier said than done.

CHAPTER FORTY-TWO

Marie – Now

I do what little I can to grit through the stinging in my eyes each tear leaves behind in their wake. With both hands bound behind my back, I have no other option but to let the salty liquid run down my cheeks.

I'm still alive. Toni sent her father off again to cool down, pulling him and his knife away from my neck. I doubt she can keep protecting me from death like this. He wants blood, and I can't help antagonizing him now that I know what happened to Tommy.

The pain returns in my shoulder as my adrenaline fades, clawing and throbbing at my skin. So much so I am forced to think about anything else while I focus on my breathing. Over the last year, I'd spent thirty minutes a day meditating. It sounds stupid, but I needed the calmness in my life whenever my anxiety went into overdrive. But no amount of focusing or letting go of the world around me could block out these last few hours.

"Come on, Marie. Just confess. Don't you want to do this the easy way?" Toni asks. She's sitting by my side on the sofa, speaking to me as if we're still friends while recording the conversation, creeping me the hell out.

"'The easy way'? You mean whatever way gets me to confess the fastest."

Toni scoffs and leans toward me. "No, I mean whatever way gets you talking without my father needing to step in."

My chest and shoulder radiate with pain for a moment as I picture Steven standing over me with his knife. I wonder how much he was enjoying making me suffer. Toni is already getting inside my head with little effort.

"If I were you, I'd want this all to be over with. Just let the truth come out and set you free from this prison you've created for yourself."

I know what she's doing, and it won't work. At least not yet. "I've been hiding in this place for five years. What makes you think I couldn't continue doing so for another five or ten or twenty years?"

Toni leans away and exhales through flared nostrils as she crosses her arms over her chest. "You know we found her, don't you?" she says changing the subject.

"Found who?" I say with a shrug.

"Sanchez's other girl. The other woman you so desperately craved to beat."

"Oh, her," I reply, my head lowering. A lump in my throat forms. I never knew her name. I avoided thinking about the possibility of Zach calling out anyone else's but my own. He was mine.

I knew there were others he'd see for a night or two, but this other person had hung around for longer than anyone else. Of course, Zach didn't hold back on letting me notice this information, the bastard. I think he made sure I realized he had options. He wanted me to play his games and compete for his love to inflate his ego. It worked like a charm.

"Yeah, you understand who I'm talking about. We had some interesting questions to ask Rose Melton."

The corner of my mouth twists up. "I don't care what she had to say," I blurt. But I realize the importance of this other woman far too late to be of use.

"Come on, you recognize who she is and why we went to the trouble of finding her, right?" Toni says. "Think about it."

I do what I can to hide my feelings, but Toni sees right through me. "Maybe, but I didn't know her. I can only confirm she was close to Zach."

"She was the one who motivated you to do the gas station robbery, wasn't she."

"Yes," I reply, squirming in my spot.

"Not only did she inspire you to make the worst decision of your life, she also testified against Zach. She too would help him rob the banks, yet the feds cut her a deal so she could also sell Zach out and go into hiding. I gotta say, the loyalty you both exhibited makes me question why either of you bothered to date him in the first place."

I shake my head, trying to forget. How does Toni know so much about this?

"Guess what we learned when we found her?"

"What?" I say, ready to snap. I already know the answer.

"She didn't kill our Tommy. See we had our search narrowed down to you and Rose. We could not work out who of Zach's girls was the one dumb enough to rob a gas station on a whim simply to impress him. The police did everything they could to suppress the identity of the shooter. That's why I moved in here. We had to keep an eye on you while my dad monitored Rose from a distance."

I turn toward her with a narrowed brow. "When was this? When did you find out the truth about me?"

"Less than a week ago. We confirmed who each of you were. And I have to say, it disappointed me. I honestly thought you weren't the one who pulled the trigger. It didn't seem like something you had in you when we first met. And no matter how close I tried to get to you, nothing about your past ever came up."

"Is that why you and your father orchestrated this whole mess? To make me talk?"

"We were sick of waiting. And I felt the only way to make your lips move was for you to believe there was a danger threatening us both. There was no way in hell you'd add the death of a young girl to your conscience after what you did to Tommy."

I stare up and away from Toni as more tears burn my eyes. "This isn't happening," I mutter to myself.

"It is though. You can't escape this. You're a killer, Marie."

"I'm not."

"Hey now, you can't fight the truth. None of us can. Instead, it's time to embrace who you are and accept what happened five years ago. Don't you want to make it to Champagne Beach?"

My eyes go wide for a moment.

"What? You thought I didn't know about that goal of yours? It wasn't hard to snoop through your computer when you were asleep. I found the spreadsheet on your desktop, not to mention the obvious wallpaper photo you always stared at. I found it interesting the way you kept extending out the money you thought you needed for the trip. Is that how you justified not taking it?"

I stare down at the cell phone as it records all of this. Toni is trying to wear me down, piece by piece, and I can feel it working. She's done her homework. She even knows some of the lies I tell myself. Do I let her win, or do I fight back, knowing the alternative involves her father slicing me open with his knife?

I continue to give her an answer when Steven comes rushing out into the living room.

"What's going on?" Toni asks.

"We have to go," he says without explanation. I can see a bag in his hand being stuffed with items that were left around my house as if he'd planned on moving in. Now they were being treated like contaminated objects that needed disposing of.

"What do you mean we have to go?" Toni asks, standing up. She brushes by me, leaving the cell unattended. I could grab it and try to hop away as I had with the other phone to call Dustin for help, but I wouldn't make it far enough to be out of the signal jammer's range.

"I've been listening to the police radio with the jammer off. One neighbor has reported my car as suspicious. The cops aren't panicked about it yet, but they plan on sending a unit by to take a quick look. They'll run the plates and work out they're fake. If that happens while we're in here, it could be game over."

I try to hide my smile, unsure what consequences there will be if Steven catches my expression in the confusion.

"Dammit," Toni mutters. "We need more time." She grabs the cell and turns off the recording. Her eyes fall to mine and confirm what I hoped wouldn't be the case. "You're coming with us."

I shake my head, desperate for this ordeal to be over. I want to go and sleep in my bed and not come out from under the covers for twelve hours.

"On your feet," Steven demands, leaning down over the sofa from behind me. "Stand by the kitchen door and don't move. Got it?"

I give him a sigh and point to my legs. "That might be harder than you think."

Steven bares his teeth at me as he ducks down and cuts the zip tie from my ankles with rough hands. He pulls me to my feet and shoves me along to the door. I continue the short journey and stop at the kitchen entrance. I could make a run for it out of the house, but Steven and Toni look too agile for my fatigued body.

As the pair goes frantically about the place, I wonder to myself which neighbor made the call. I know they each have their quirks and wouldn't enjoy having an unknown vehicle sitting in the street, but this feels quick even for them.

Toni has fewer things to worry about bringing along, seeing as she supposedly lives with me. Somehow though I think our living arrangement has run its course.

"Grab some food. This might take a while," Steven says to Toni. She brushes by me into the kitchen. Opening the refrigerator as if I'm invisible, she pulls out the few items we have left from our meager supplies.

"Where are we going?" I ask. "I have the right to know."

"Don't worry," she replies. "You just concentrate on not causing us any more problems."

CHAPTER FORTY-THREE

Toni – Then

My mother died. My dad and I both found her lifeless body lying on her back in bed. The only reason we discovered her was because she hadn't emerged from her bedroom in days.

Dad had been sleeping on the couch for some time. All he and Mom seemed to do was argue, so he gave her the space she required during a tough point in their marriage. The harsh truth was they couldn't stand to be around each other at a stage when she needed him the most.

Mom started drinking alone when Tommy officially passed. On top of the liquor, she took extra doses of Valium along with antidepressants the doctor had prescribed her. The combination rapidly wore her down to the point where her system shut down overnight and never recovered. She died in her sleep, over medicating on a particularly difficult night the way a washed-up Hollywood actress did. But we weren't in Tinseltown. No reporters were going to flock to our front doorstep and demand to know the truth. This was in the real world.

It wasn't until I banged on Mom's door, begging to talk, that Dad and I both realized there was a problem. I went to her room, deciding enough was enough, that she needed to come out and face the world like the rest of us. It was the only way we'd climb out of the hole we had crawled into as a family.

Instead, I found her cold body. My voice choked up when I tried to scream, cry, and yell all at once. My mother had accidentally killed herself trying to avoid facing the pain that Tommy's absence left behind. She'd done the same to Dad and me in the process. I couldn't have had more of a range of emotions to attempt to make sense of what had happened in that moment.

One minute, I was beyond inconsolable with a damp sadness that felt like it would never go away. The next, I was furious at my mom for being so irresponsible with alcohol and her over-prescribed medicine. Her doctor would have some questions to answer.

Six weeks after seeing Dad and five other people lower Tommy's tiny casket into the earth, I had to witness my mother's burial right beside him in the family plot. Once again, I would be forced to work over the stages of grief and somehow find the means to continue through my growing hell. But how could I do so without Mom by my side to help me through the worst time in my life?

All the relatives stared at Dad and I at the funeral, probably wondering who would die next between the two of us. Their faces only confirmed my suspicions as we thanked each individual for coming.

They offered the usual comforting lines as I shook hands and hugged each attendee. "If there's anything I can do to help, just let me know," or, "I'm so sorry for your loss." I absorbed them all, feeling numb to my core with every word spoken. None of them meant any of it. There would be no support other than a few weeks of ready-made meals neither Dad nor I would want to eat.

What were we supposed to do next? Losing Tommy was a devastating enough blow to the system. Losing Mom shortly after seemed cruel. I could only imagine what was going through Dad's head. He'd lost his wife and baby boy.

The days crawled by as I floated around the house, trying to do what I could to keep it tidy. Dad had shut down and locked himself away in his study. I should have been concerned that he might develop a similar habit to Mom, but I possessed zero energy to talk about it. All of my focus went into what household chores I could handle on my own.

Finally, my dad emerged from his study beyond a need to use the bathroom or grab a beer. He came out to locate me and show me something I hadn't seen on his face in a long while: a smile. Confused, I sat him down at the kitchen table and called for him to talk without leaving the room.

"We will find her," he said.

"Find who?" I asked, puzzled and worried at the same time.

"The one who tore this family apart. The one who shot Tommy in the gas station."

"She's a woman? How did you—?"

"The shooter wore a mask, but I could tell straight away it was female."

"Wait," I said. "Does that mean you've seen the security footage?"

He nodded.

My eyes fell to the floor wondering how hard that must have been. "Did you see Tommy...?" I trailed off, not wanting to complete my thought.

"Yeah. I saw when he, you know, got hit."

I shook my head, trying not to throw up thinking about it. I needed to change the subject fast. "I thought the police stated their main suspect wasn't behind it and that they had no more leads."

Dad chuckled, but not happily, more of an angry feeling he was doing his best to conceal. "Turns out that was all a bunch of lies. I don't know what they're trying to cover up, but I finally got my hands on the security footage. It's clearly a woman on their firing at the store clerk. Her face is covered, but we will find her."

"A woman?" I asked again. "You're positive?" We all assumed the robber was male. It was usually the way these things went. The police had been nothing but vague about the shooting. None of the detectives would give us any information when we begged for it either.

"Yes. I promise you. You'll see it when I show you the recording."

I tried to take in what he was saying. He sounded half insane the way he was going about the whole thing. I didn't know if I should have continued to ask him questions or tell him he needed help. My curiosity won out. "Okay, so you've got this masked woman on camera who killed Tommy. How do you find her?"

"Simple," he said with a wide smile as he leaned back, arms crossed. "We work out who the man is in the recording who rushed into the gas station two seconds after she shot Tommy and dragged her out of there. If we get to him, we'll identify her."

I stared at Dad unsure how I was supposed to react to his manic behavior. Was this his way of dealing with Mom's death? If only we could afford therapy, I'd drag both of us to a session every week. Dad more so than me, but he'd never go.

I continued to listen to his plans and how he thought he might find this man in the recording to get to Tommy's shooter. It was all I could do to keep him talking to me outside the depths of his study. Granted, the topic didn't make for the best of conversations, it was still Dad and I speaking more than three words to each other.

I could only hope this obsession wouldn't consume him and become the new norm.

CHAPTER FORTY-FOUR

Marie – Now

I get shuffled to the SUV in a hurry through a warm nighttime breeze. It's a pleasant feeling on my face compared to the stuffy air I'd been breathing in and out all night inside. In this abrupt moment, I feel relaxed and almost forget where I am.

The rear passenger door to Steven's car opens. I am placed into the back seat of the immaculate vehicle by Toni while Steven hangs back for a minute. Toni applies a second wrist zip tie restraint to me for strength and then ducks down to rebind my ankles. She keeps her eyes on me while her dad runs inside my house for the last few things he'd brought along for this trip, including the signal jammer.

It's only a small box, but that damn thing gave me hell when I thought Steven was one of Zach's goons sent to kill me. I have to admit Toni played her part as Beth to perfection when she freaked out about her cell losing its capability to get online.

With the jammer offline and out of my way, an opportunity presented itself. All I have in my possession is the knife I had planned on burying into Steven's neck when the time came. I could cut away my zip ties when no one is looking and escape out the car. Of course, I first have to break through the child-locked doors and windows I saw Toni engage.

My only other plan to survive tonight involves getting in contact with Dustin somehow so he can send the cavalry running my way to arrest these people. It wasn't a possibility before with the signal jammer. Now, all I need to do is get my hands on a cell.

I have his number memorized. I could even shoot him a text to start the ball rolling.

As we rush away from my house, I want to ask more than anything else where we're going, but I recognize that question will fall on deaf ears. I don't know if this is part of a contingency plan or if it's a kneejerk reaction Steven is having. Either way, I'm heading further into the unknown.

What if they run me out to the desert and kill me? What if they drag me across the border to Mexico, never to return? I let the wild thoughts consume me as per usual. There's no point in trying to regulate my anxiety. Things have progressed too far beyond my command over the last day for me to think rationally about the world.

"Take the next left," Toni says.

I push up on my wrists and realize she is using the cell to guide them to a certain stop. I don't understand what to make of that information. Plus, her screen sits past where I can fully see to learn the desired location ahead.

I can't help but wonder why Toni isn't driving with Steven working me over in the back seat like some form of mobile torture chamber. It seems to be a wasted opportunity, but I won't let them in on my sick idea. All I hope from my observation is that Toni still has control of the situation or at least enough pull to stop her dad from taking things too far as he had before. My shoulder throbs with the thought.

I slump against the window and try to take in dying views of downtown as we head toward the industrial side of the municipality. Less and less housing barrios fill the area as the smell of oil and steel consume my senses. A bump in the road tells me we've crossed over from the outskirts of the city to a commercial park. Soon, the three of us will be alone again.

Steven pulls the car into a gravel-covered lot off a street littered with cracks. A sign in the front warns all about trespassing or dumping trash in both English and Spanish. I glance left and right and see more of these empty lots interspersed with factories and the occasional house. Could I run to one of these places and find someone inside to help me? It seems unlikely at this hour.

"Kill the lights," Toni says over Steven's shoulder. He does so and shuts off the engine. And just like that, we blend into the background. There's no person around for miles, but I can still hear the city in the distance, along with the sounds of the distant highways.

Toni holds out the cell she used to guide us here. I spot a near identical one within the bag. It must be the water-damaged unit. I wonder if it has dried out enough to function. I only need to make a quick call.

"We have little time if we're planning to get her talking with only words," Steven says like I don't exist.

"I'm aware," she says. "I'll call out to you when I'm done."

I try not to let my confusion interrupt their 'private' conversation. What's Toni going to do when we're alone?

Steven climbs out of the car and heads around to Toni's rear door. She winds the window down with the press of a button. What more do they have to say to each other? I see him rummaging through a separate bag from Toni's until he pulls out a second handgun.

The revolver gets placed into Toni's hand as casually as anything else would. It's not the same type of weapon Steven has on him. Maybe a backup? I feel a lump in my throat take over just looking at it, forcing me to press my body hard against the door. Toni puts the gun away into her backpack and zips it up. What does she need it for?

She turns to me with her fake and friendly smile, the one that can read my mind. "Don't worry," she says. "He doesn't trust you to be alone with me in such a tight space. If you do as you're told though, I won't ever have to touch it."

I give her a rushed smile, not wanting her to realize how scared I am. I only hope she doesn't use the weapon to get me talking.

I'm forced to think about my day in court against Zach. My testimony contributed strongly to him going away for life. I still remember standing outside the courtroom with Dustin as the DA coached me on exactly what to say. One wrong word and the deal was off the table. I'd go back to facing several charges that would see me locked up in a tiny jail cell until the day I died.

It was either Zach or me. I couldn't have gone to jail. I wouldn't have made it longer than a few days on the inside.

Toni snaps me out of my thoughts by clicking her fingers in front of my eyes, instantly reminding me I'm a prisoner of a different kind.

CHAPTER FORTY-FIVE

Toni – Then

Two years went by. It was hard to fathom that time could flow at a normal rate after my mother passed away, but somehow, against our wishes, life moved on. At least it did for the people around us. For Dad and me though, each day was as trying and as long as the last.

I continued to live at home to be close to Dad, putting my studies on hold indefinitely. He needed me there to keep him from hitting rock bottom. Whether he cared to admit to it, he was depressed and broken, and only someone who understood the pain daily life had become could help.

Every day when I woke up, for a short moment, I thought I was back in high school. My parents had preserved my room in such a way it was easy for my delicate mind to believe so. My eyes would wander the space in a half-dazed confusion, convinced for a split second I was in a better age when my mom and brother were still alive. Then my brain would pull the rug from under my feet to force me to remember. I could see why Mom chose to slip away into the darkness. Reality was too much to bear on a good day.

Dad hadn't worked a day since Mom's funeral, not that I blamed him. We were living off a combination of my part-time job at the coffee shop and what remained of my parents' savings. My mom left Dad everything in her will, most of which he already had access to. The only extra money we got was from her 401k, and we were going to need it. I couldn't predict how long we could maintain this course. It became my burden to get Dad out of his rut and back to work.

Before our lives were torn apart, my dad still worked as an EMT. He relied upon Mom's income as a librarian to support the household, meaning our budget took a big hit when Tommy came along. Dad loved working from the back of an ambulance despite the challenges and various difficulties it threw his way. The horror stories I'd heard when I was old enough to hear them made me wonder why he put up with such a job. It only added to the invincible image I already had of Dad. Nothing in this world could break him. That was until he found Tommy shot in the chest in a Long Beach gas station.

He could have been the world's best surgeon when he discovered my brother. It still wouldn't have saved the little guy from an induced coma the way the bullet had bounced off a bone in his chest to hit him in the skull. I shuddered anytime I thought about what that would have been like for my dad to find, considering the dozens of gunshot victims he had treated over the ten plus years of his career. I doubted he would ever be an EMT again.

Despite knowing Tommy would never be the same, he did everything he could to help. My mother had told me that the responding EMTs had to pull Dad out of the way when they reached the scene. All the while, I was only a short distance away, celebrating the end of the semester with my friends instead of flying home to see my family.

If it wasn't for me and my selfish attitude, Tommy would have still been alive, my mother would have never died of an overdose, and Dad wouldn't be a shell of a person who hid in his study day and night.

I rarely saw my father come up for air from the tiny room. Back when things were normal, he kept the door open in that space and didn't mind being interrupted. The office was only supposed to be used for tasks like paying bills, organizing important paperwork for the family, or for Dad to do any extra medical studies his job often required.

Now he lived in there, keeping it locked, with the curtains shut and the light off. I could see only the glare from his laptop under the crack of the door if I squinted hard enough. What he got up to in there was a mystery. But whatever it was, it didn't make us any money. It seemed to only drain his bank account even further.

I'd been given access to most of his accounts to pay all the bills he was too distracted to handle. In fact, I took over taking care of the household. I cleaned, managed our funds, and made the meals all while trying to work as many hours as I could waitressing to keep money coming in.

It would not be sufficient long term. I didn't make enough per hour to cover even half our expenses, and my tips were lousy. I figured it had something to do with my mood. My shifts never started with a smile, and I was often ready for a stiff drink by the end of a long day. Fortunately, my boss understood what my family had gone through and allowed me to keep working for him.

The coffee shop only served an all-day breakfast and lunch, meaning I would get home before six if I did a full shift. After that many hours of public interaction, I was wiped out but still had to look after the house my dad had spent his time ignoring. He'd pile up his dishes in the sink, not tidy any crumbs left on the bench, and make a mess in the refrigerator. I could ask him nicely or yell until I was blue in the face for him to clean up after himself, but it wouldn't change his actions. He was not the parent I once knew.

I'd spend a solid two hours each night cleaning and making sure everything was in order before I could relax and take a moment for myself. My parents had decided they'd had enough of being responsible adults the second we lost Tommy. My mother elected to drown her pain with alcohol and pills until she died while my dad stopped living. I had no choice but to pick up the slack and keep who was left in our family going. After several years though, the rut was becoming a deep trench.

We'd fallen into a stalemate existence with no sign of reform coming soon. I couldn't leave my father like this without severe consequence. And to make things worse, none of our relatives lived close enough to offer more than a superficial bit of help. Our lives would not improve unless something drastic happened.

Change came our way more than two years after someone killed Tommy. I counted his death to be the moment the bullet entered his tiny body and not six months later after we'd spent countless hours staring at what was left of him. He wasn't alive during that time. Modern medicine gave us false hope he was still in there.

I remembered the night my dad emerged from the office a lot earlier than he ever would as if it were yesterday. He normally wouldn't emerge until midnight to stumble off to bed for a few hours of sleep before he'd rise at four or five in the early morning to start his day of darkness in the study again. This time, he charged straight up to me on the sofa as I attempted to focus on some terrible reality TV show.

"I've done it," Dad said.

"Done what?" I asked. I looked him up and down. His faded clothing was covered in stains. His long hair was a mess, and his stubble had reached a point of becoming a beard. Still, I was happy to be exchanging more than simple grunts of communication.

He smiled at me as I switched the TV set off. "I've found him."

"Found who?" I asked, wondering what level of crazy my question would generate.

"The man in the gas station. The one who pulled the woman away after she shot Tommy. I've finally got him."

CHAPTER FORTY-SIX

Marie – Now

My eyes dart from Toni to the backpack she has at her feet. There's a loaded gun inside, waiting to be utilized. Is she planning on executing me the second we're finished with whatever this is? Or will the revolver be her last resort to extract the confession out of me for a second time in one night?

I don't know what I'll do if she jams that weapon in my face and threatens to pull the trigger. Death may seem like the better option over confessing my past again on camera, but I still value living too much to give up.

The thought makes me think about the cell I attempted to destroy earlier tonight. I know it's also in the same backpack as the gun. I saw Toni pack it. Why would she do such a thing if it were broken and unusable? Too many questions swim around my brain as usual.

"I'm sorry about all this," Toni says.

My eyes land on hers, unsure what she means. Is she sorry for dragging me out in the car or for this whole ordeal she and her father have thrown upon me? I don't clarify, not wanting to upset things. Toni seems calmer now we are away from the house.

"It's okay," I mutter.

Toni gives me a flash of a smile as she plays with the second cell again. She spins the device around in her hand as if lost in thought.

I know what she has planned for me. "This again," I say.

"Yes, this again." Toni holds the phone tight and taps away.

I hear the sound effect used to indicate a video is being recorded and realize Toni is planning on holding the spare cell. This can only be a good thing in my mind. With one arm otherwise occupied, she will be less capable of torturing me.

"So, where were we?" she asks, picking up from our last conversation. I avoid her eyes for a moment and look out the window to see Steven smoking a cigarette in the distance. I wonder how long he's been craving that hit of nicotine. He doesn't come across as a smoker.

"Has he always done that?" I ask Toni while I point a finger out the car.

"What? Smoked? No. It started when the stress of trying to find a woman in witness protection got to be too much for him."

"I'm sorry," I say. "I didn't mean to—"

"It's fine. You didn't know."

I honestly didn't. I couldn't smell it on his breath when I had him in my face multiple times, demanding I confess. He must have been holding out as long as he could.

"Anyway, that's not why we're here," she says, making sure the camera is level.

My heart flutters for a moment. Toni will do what is necessary to get this confession out of me. But I still have one move to play to stop that from happening. The problem is whether I can execute it or not.

"What is your name?" she says ignoring me. It's the same question Steven tried on me.

"Are you serious?" I blurt with a lack of control.

"It's a simple question. Who are you?"

"Karen Rainey," I say, certain she will punish me for using my WitSec profile again.

"How about this: what is your real name?"

Her eyes lock onto mine like a guided missile while her brow narrows in, ready for a verbal assault should I answer in a manner that won't please her.

"Well? What is it?"

"Marie. Marie Williams. That's my actual name."

"Was that so hard? Now tell me, Marie, where you are from? Where did you grow up?"

"Chino, California." The words fall out of my mouth. This is what she wants.

"Good. So, what brings you all the way out here then? Seems a bit far away from home."

Before the gas station, I lived in Norwalk, California. It wasn't far from where I grew up and gave me access to everything Los Angeles could offer. After spending a year in a WitSec house in Palm Springs, unable to contact a single person I knew, Dustin told me he got me a place in Phoenix, Arizona that would be ideal to lie low in for a few years.

I never wanted to move to Arizona. Being out of Cali only made me miss Chino more so than I already had. Every day I think about the dairy farms that were beautifully interspersed between the industrial areas and the dense urban sprawl. Sure, Phoenix is only a short flight away from home, but it's not the same when the people you once knew all think you are dead.

"Well?" Toni asks.

I shrug, coming back to her question. She knows why I'm out here. "The same reason you and your dad are out here." I study her eyes and don't see a reaction. She is doing well to contain herself. Do I keep pushing?

"We'll get back to that one. How about you tell me what you do for work then? Do you have a job?"

"Three. At least I had three. Not so sure they'll still be there for me after today though."

Toni ignores my remark and continues, guilt free. "And what were these jobs?"

"I am, or was, a VA. A Virtual Assistant. I managed emails, schedules, and so on for a few executives who needed someone to do the tasks they couldn't be bothered doing."

"And you did this from home?"

I let my breath come out of my flaring nostrils. "Yes, from home. From my study as you know. Or as Beth did."

The mention of the name Beth causes a slight twitch in Toni's face, but she continues. "So you live far away from where you grew up and earn money doing a job that a person could perform from their home. Correct?"

"Yes. Is there a point to all of this?"

Toni doesn't budge an inch. "I'm just establishing who you are."

"So you can get my confession and put it online for the world to digest, right?"

Silence.

"Am I right?" I ask.

"Don't you want the people to understand the real you? Wouldn't you prefer to give them a chance to find out that what you did was an accident?"

I shift backward in the seat to the car window. She hadn't believed me when I told her the shooting was an accident. Is this a trick? Or is she defending my actions? What game is she playing?

"Well?"

I struggle to speak. My throat feels like it won't open, so I try to clear it.

"Marie?"

"Yes," I blurt. "I want them to know, to understand, I never, in a thousand years, meant for it to happen."

"Meant for what to happen?" Toni asks, leaning in.

I close my eyes and feel the torment stirring within. My answer wants to come out to be recorded on camera for the world to see, but in the same moment, I consider all the hatred that will forever fly in my direction. I have to focus on the plan.

She gets in closer again, placing one arm on my shoulder. "You can do this, Marie. Think of how liberating it will be to let the truth out."

I nod to her. "You're right," I say, closing my eyes for a second. All the while, my hands have been inching over to my pocket as one. Toni is leaning over me, her neck exposed. All I need to do is grab out the tiny blade I still have in my possession and plunge it deep into her throat. By the time she realizes what has happened, I can get to the gun in the backpack and shoot her father outside as he draws on his final cigarette.

"Marie?" Toni says, pulling me from my dark fantasy. I gaze into her eyes and see her little brother staring back at me. As much as I want to survive, to escape this hell, I can't be the one to bring any more harm to the Price family.

Can I?

CHAPTER FORTY-SEVEN

Toni – Then

Dad typed away on his laptop, preparing to show me something I had a feeling would only make me nauseous. I didn't want to pursue some criminal friend of the woman who killed Tommy. My only focus was to keep our heads above water—a task I was barely achieving on a good day.

Dad swiveled his computer around in my direction. My mouth fell open and got covered by my hand when I saw what appeared to be security footage from the gas station where Tommy got shot. I slammed my eyes shut. "You're not going to show me—"

"It's okay. You won't see him. I cropped Tommy out of the image."

"Are you sure? I don't want to look at it ever. Do you understand?"

"Of course I do. Do you think I wanted to experience this? Watching my boy—your brother—be shot on some grainy surveillance camera just so we could find this guy?"

I slowly opened my eyes, lowering my hand aside from my face. "I'm sorry, Dad. I can only imagine how horrible that must have been."

He shook his head and glanced at the screen in thought. "It's like falling into your worst nightmare without having a way to wake up again."

I grabbed his elbow to bring him back from whatever dark place his mind had slipped to. "Show me who this guy is. That's why we're watching this, right?"

"Yeah," he said, anger brewing. Dad paused for a moment longer and played the footage to me. I saw the woman who shot

Tommy kneeling down at the end of an aisle moments before a man rushed in through the front door of the store. His eyes stopped on where Tommy's body would be only for a moment until he noticed the woman. Anger swelled in my core as I watched her be aided out of the gas station in a rush while Tommy laid wounded off screen.

"Who is this piece of crap?" I asked.

"Zachary Sanchez. He's a wanted criminal. A bank robber to be specific."

"A bank robber? Are you serious?"

"Deadly so. He's connected to more than a dozen robberies across the state of California alone."

"So where is he now?"

"United States Penitentiary, Florence, Colorado."

"Prison?" I asked, standing up and away from the tablet. I'd seen enough. "What are you talking about?"

"He's in a federal penitentiary. Specifically, he's locked up within a supermax unit serving a life sentence. Apparently, since he went inside, he turned violent and killed his cellmate. They had to transfer him to this hellhole to keep him contained."

I gawked at Dad with my mouth open.

"You wouldn't believe the trouble I had getting this information."

My hands landed on my hips. "You didn't do anything illegal, did you?"

"Don't worry, okay? All I did was pay the right people. It's just security footage after all."

I held my pose and watched his eyes. "Fine. But promise me you won't do something stupid and get locked up yourself. I can't lose you as well."

"Hey, come on." Dad pulled me in for a hug, "I'm not going anywhere ever. You're stuck with me, kiddo."

I squeezed him tight, wishing we weren't bothering with all of this, but at the same time I was starting to understand why Dad was so obsessed with finding the truth.

HE'S AT YOUR DOOR

"So," Dad said, drawing away. "Seeing as they locked Zach up in a supermax, it makes us meeting him a little challenging."

"What do you mean? Like, if we went in as visitors?"

"Yep. These prisoners aren't as accessible as your average inmate. I've also heard that a guard will listen in on the conversation."

"So what do we do? He obviously has information on the woman in the video."

"Exactly. That's what makes this so damn frustrating. It's like she disappeared that night and only he knows why. I swear she's a ghost."

I paced about the carpet of the dining room, trying my hardest not to bite my nails. "Maybe she's dead."

Dad's brow screwed up at my suggestion.

"Well, think about it. She shot a kid inside a gas station and forced Zachary—a bank robber—to rush in and have his face recorded on a security camera. He probably drove her out to the desert and killed her. I'll bet it's one of the charges he's facing."

Dad closed the recording and pulled up a document on the tablet. "According to this, there are only two major bank robbery charges against him that the courts could convict him on. They ignored every other felony or crime he committed on the outside because of a lack of compelling evidence. He did, however, kill his cellmate after his trial. So it's not impossible to assume he might have killed her. If only, right?"

"Are you serious?" I asked, certain I didn't hear him.

"Just talking out loud. I know it's not right to wish she were dead, but some days the thought of it gets me through."

A minute of silence clouded the air between us. I'd never seen this side of my father before. Worried for his mental health, I continued the conversation.

"Okay then. The two robberies he got charged for. What happened? Was he sloppy?"

"Not at all. They were textbook and perfect like the rest. But there was something each had in common that the feds used to bring him down."

I shrugged.

"Each case had a female eyewitness who pretended to be a customer of the bank. They robbed the banks alongside Zachary. Both women weren't a normal part of his operation. Can you guess who one of these people was?"

I stared at the table for a moment in thought until it hit me. "The woman who shot Tommy?"

"The very same. I have the names of both girls who testified against Zachary Sanchez. They got kept from the public record, but after a bit of digging I found them."

I felt a mix of excitement and terror flood my stomach. "What are their names?"

"Rose Melton and Marie Williams. Both are now in lower levels of witness protection."

My eyes narrowed. "You're kidding. How can they have been witnesses if they were a part of the robbery?"

"Neither handled a weapon or gave any orders. They simply kept a lookout and watched the bank managers via secret signals. It's all been caught on security footage."

I scoffed. "What a pair of idiots. Why'd they do it?"

Dad pursed his lips. "My guess is they were adrenaline junkies along for the ride, each infatuated with some bank-robbing idiot. What does that tell you?"

I shrugged and tried my best not to get frustrated. "That they were swayed to do something stupid."

"A good thought there, but what it explains is why our shooter disappeared."

"What do you mean?" I asked, arms crossed firm.

"Simple. She cut a deal. Someone urged her to testify against Zachary or face the full brunt of the law over Tommy's shooting."

I gripped the nearest dining room chair in a flash to stop myself from falling over. "Are you saying she got away with it?"

"Nothing else makes sense. All this time we've been chasing a ghost. This woman should be in prison for her part in the bank robbery alone, so to not be charged for what she did at the gas station would take something as big as testifying against a dangerous criminal."

I found myself with both hands on the dining room chair for stability. It was a lot to accept, even on a good day. I stood there trying to wrap my head around it all until one thought blared out at me. "Wait," I said, looking at my dad in the eyes. "You mentioned they convicted this Zach guy of two separate crimes."

"That's right. And both cases were near identical. Each witness who testified against him was a woman. Both were, at some point, his girlfriend. The feds used these morons to bring him down in flames for one bank robbery each."

"Then they made them state witnesses," I muttered.

"Bingo. Two female eyewitnesses: Rose Melton and Marie Williams. Two cases. Both ended the same way. One of them had to have killed our Tommy and caused your mother to drive herself to those damn pills."

I shook my head as a surge of emotions flooded my system until anger won. "So how do we figure out who murdered Tommy?"

CHAPTER FORTY-EIGHT

Marie – Now

Toni continues to push me with her questions, trying her finest to get specifics out of me. But once I've decided I can't go through with my desperate plan, I pull back from the conversation, put up my walls, and try to shut her out as best as I can. My knife remains hidden.

"I don't understand you, Marie. One moment you seem ready to open up and tell me everything. The next, you're closing down on me. Why?" Toni places the cell up onto the rear shelf of the SUV and keeps it recording and pointed at us.

She sits across from me in the backseat of her father's ride. Steven's outside, still smoking, on his second cigarette as if one stick wasn't sufficient.

I keep my eyes low and focused on the floor so Toni can't engage me the way she'd like to. It's angering the hell out of her, but for now I've made my decision not to hurt her or her father. I can't ruin their lives any more than I already have.

I will still do what I can to escape this mess though. It will just have to involve luck and timing to execute the only other plan that comes to mind.

"Not answering me, huh? That's not a smart play, especially when you know who's waiting for you outside of this car." She makes a thumb over her shoulder toward her dad. He's gotten rough with me tonight, not holding back on physical violence to get me to talk. If this entire endeavor were up to him, he'd have already cut me until the truth bled out. My body would have been dropped off somewhere in the desert by now. The feeling is impossible to ignore.

"You don't want things to reach that point again, do you, Marie? I saw that look of fear in your eyes when I came out and stopped him."

I lift myself as a thought hits my brain, one that will get Toni upset where I need her. "You knew your dad would do that though, didn't you? You wanted him to stab me."

Toni shakes her head. "It's not like that." She leans in closer. "I promise."

She's playing good cop, bad cop with me, acting out each role. That much is as plain as day. "I know it is. You hate me with every fiber in your being. This is all an act to lure me in and break down my walls. You want me to confess everything and suffer the consequences. Then, you'll pull the trigger on that gun you have tucked away there, just like your father wants you to."

Toni's mouth is agape with a slight tremble as she stares at me. I've struck something deep within. Her fists clench as her eyes shut tight. Here we go.

"You don't know what you're talking about." The back of her hand comes flying out and slaps me hard across the face quicker than I expect. A tearing sensation slices through my skin, worse than it should. My hands lift to my cheek and touch the numb area. When my fingers draw away, the tips are coated in blood. I look to Toni to see an old ring on the hand that slapped me. A decent-sized diamond pokes out into the world like a dagger.

Toni's breathing speeds up with the rage inside her she has been trying to contain this entire week. There's no point her holding back now.

"Where did you get that rock from?" I ask.

"Never you mind."

"No, no. It looks expensive and not really something a person your age would wear. Was it your grandmother's? An auntie maybe?" I study her face and see it twitch. "No, someone closer."

"It was my mom's ring, okay?"

"Was?" I ask without thinking.

"Yeah, was. She's dead. She died in her sleep mixing too many pills and alcohol together, all because she was struggling to drown out the pain of losing her little boy."

My heart skips a beat. I had no idea what happened to her mother. I knew she existed back when Dustin offered me the deal, but that was the first and last time she ever entered my thoughts. Learning she overdosed on pills and alcohol because I shot her kid only sends another solid brick of guilt down into my core. But I can't let that stop me. I should be on the floor, begging for Toni's forgiveness, but I'm trying to survive. And the only way forward is to push this girl into a corner.

"She'd be ashamed of you if she saw what you two were up to."

Her hand flies out again. I flinch but don't feel a thing. She restrained herself, seeing the blood on my face. Her tensed shoulders drop. I can see she will lose angered momentum unless I keep poking for her emotions to take control. It's my only hope.

"I must be on the money, huh? This whole time you've wanted to beat me senseless, just like dear old dad."

Toni's eyes narrow in. Giving me the information I need.

"That's right. You convince yourself that you're nothing like him, that you won't let the rage seize you, but—"

"Shut up!" she yells. "I'm not like that."

"Oh, really? Because I think I'm onto something here. This little fact pains you, doesn't it. Like psycho father, like psycho daughter. Your poor mother." I tsk at Toni twice.

Toni's eyes clench tight again as she tries to push me out by holding her palms to her head. "Shut up," she whispers, edging closer to a meltdown.

"Admit it," I press. "You can't control yourself."

A second later, her hands dig into the backpack and pull out the pistol. "Just shut your damn mouth!" she yells as she points the gun at my face.

I do as told while keeping my eyes locked onto Toni's. She's pulled the revolver out exactly as I want her to. Now, I have to tread lightly and pray that Steven is far enough away to not hear our exchange.

Toni's breathing is as ragged as her shaking arm that's aiming the gun at my head. She bares her teeth as if she wants to take a bite out of me. I've never seen her want me dead so much while also doing what she can to hold back. One wrong move, and a bullet will end my life.

"So you understand how to shut up now. Amazing," Toni says through a half-clenched jaw.

"I guess so." It's enough of a response to keep her angry while hopefully not sending her over the edge.

"Well then, seeing as you can't be silenced, it's time you talked. What did you do to my brother? What did you do to Tommy Price?"

I'd almost forgotten her cell was recording all of this from the shelf of the rear window. Is she really trying to go for a confession now? All anyone will see is an angry woman holding a gun to my head. Anything I admit won't be taken seriously.

"I don't know what you're talking about," I say.

"Don't bullshit me!" she yells. "Tell me the truth." She presses the weapon closer. I understand this thing is loaded and ready to fire in the hands of an emotionally stressed person, but I have to continue with my plan.

"What did you do to my brother? One more lie and I swear to god I'll—"

"Okay, I'll talk. Just lower that down please."

She doesn't comply straight away, but after a moment of thought, the gun lowers enough so it's no longer in my face. Toni keeps her focus on me while gripping the weapon. "Speak."

"You win," I say, ready to make my move. "Your brother. I walked into the gas station that night and..." I shift my eyes from Toni to her father outside and frown.

Toni glances in that direction and gazes at her dad in confusion, long enough for me to snatch the revolver clean out of her control. She tries to grab it back, but I elbow her away by turning sideways with a quick strike. The cell phone falls to the floor in the scuffle as I get a solid grip on the weapon.

"Don't move." I point the gun at her chest. I hate having this object in my fingers. It only reminds me of the horrible thing I did to this girl's family. But I have no choice but to wield it and take over if I want to escape.

Toni doesn't budge or make a sound. She appreciates what I'm capable of. She knows the wreck I've become.

With her under control, all that's left is to get out of the car and ensure Steven won't catch wind of the situation and shoot me.

What could go wrong?

CHAPTER FORTY-NINE

Toni – Then

We hit a wall. We were positive Dad had worked out there were two women who could have shot Tommy, but we didn't know who out of Rose Melton and Marie Williams was guilty. To make matters worse, both girls were in witness protection with fresh pseudonyms, living in what could be any part of the country. We needed to visit Zachary Sanchez in prison to work out which girl he pulled from the gas station that night.

We couldn't just go to the federal jail directly. Dad feared the moment we checked into the front desk someone would notify the US marshals. How would we explain our presence there? Zach was one of a few select people who knew the identity of Tommy's shooter. We needed a way in that wouldn't see us held up for hours of questioning.

Three months passed with no solution coming to light. I could tell it was killing Dad on the inside to be so close to the truth while also being as far away as possible from getting the next piece of the puzzle.

"Come on, damn it!" he yelled at his laptop.

We were sitting at the breakfast bar in the kitchen having lunch. I'd gotten him to bring his computer out from his study for a few hours a day so he wouldn't stay hidden inside that dank room for weeks on end. I told him he had to look after himself a lot more, otherwise I would force him to speak to a therapist. Reluctantly, he'd agreed to try.

"What's wrong?" I asked as I sipped an espresso while browsing on my phone. I was about to head off for an afternoon shift at the coffee shop.

"Nothing," he muttered.

"It sounds like something. What is it?"

Dad let a long breath flow out through his nostrils. "It's nothing. Just thought I had a lead is all."

"What did you find?" I asked.

"A name of a US Marshal who could have been handling the girls."

"That's good, isn't it?"

"It is, but I can't confirm what he had to do with Zachary's case. These files I paid for are all locked up. We have to bribe someone higher up the chain than a desk clerk if we ever want to find something decent."

Dad no longer said things like "I have to, or I should do this." Instead, he always said "we" and thought of us as a team. Father and daughter. We were both obsessed with one topic: finding Tommy's killer. Any sin committed in the process would reflect upon us both.

"So, what was the US Marshal's name?"

Dad glanced at his screen. I could see his eyes darting left and right over and over until he saw the man mentioned again. "Deputy US Marshal Dustin Taylor."

I shrugged to myself. "What makes you think he had anything to do with the girls?"

"That's just it. I know he had to be involved with at least one of them. Maybe both. His name is all over the sign-in log for every court date Sanchez had."

"He was probably watching the case to get a feel for Sanchez as a person to see how badly either girl needed the witness protection." I ceased talking as my brain took over with another thought. "Were there any other US Marshals signing in during that time?"

Dad's eyes scanned away. His fingers danced over the keyboard, searching for an answer to my question. He stopped typing. "None. Just Deputy US Marshal Dustin Taylor."

Our minds met for a brief second as we each came to the same conclusion at once. I spoke first. "He was working both cases. Both girls."

Dad nodded as his mouth curled into a half smile. "He had to have been. Why else was he there?"

"If it's true, how do we locate this guy?"

Dad slumped a little in his chair. His happy face faded along with any hope I had just found.

"That's the thing. Finding him is a piece of cake. He's a government employee. I could call his desk phone now."

"So, why don't you?"

He shook his head. "As soon as he works out who I am, he won't have a word to say to me. In fact, he'll probably send a few officers out to pick me up for a 'voluntary' interview just for speaking with him. Not something we need."

My hand found its way to my forehead. That was it. We couldn't visit Zach at the prison. We couldn't speak to the US Marshal who handled the girls. We'd never find Tommy's killer. Not without some luck. "This is such bullshit."

"Hey, it's okay," Dad said. "We'll figure out another angle."

"No, we won't!" I yelled, slapping printouts Dad had stacked on the bench. The papers flew into the air and took their time fluttering about as they fell to the tiles below.

A gentle arm found its way to my shoulder. "Come on, honey. Let's forget this thing for a moment and try to relax, huh?"

"Relax?" I scoffed. "How the hell do you think I can ever loosen up and not let this bother me? I'm about to start another shift at the coffee shop. When that's over, I need to run home and make you dinner, clean the house, and sort out the bills while you hide in the study some more."

His hand cowered in silence as I breathed hard. I could almost feel the guilt and shame he'd no doubt be feeling radiating out. Either that, or he was too broken to argue with me anymore.

He had let his life be consumed by the loss of his son and wife. I doubt it ever occurred to him that he still had a daughter who needed him to be there for her. Every moment he spent trying to pin down Tommy's killer only made him less of a father.

We remained silent. I tried to sip my coffee, but it tasted sour. A moment later, I slid off the high stool and grabbed my cell, leaving my drink where it sat. I would be tidying up the house as soon as I got home, so there was no point in taking it to the sink.

"I have to go," I muttered over my shoulder as I strolled away.

"I'm sorry," Dad said.

Stopping at the edge of the room, I faced him. He'd never once apologized for the way he treated me. He never thanked me for the meals I prepared him. Never did he acknowledge the effort I put in around the house or the sacrifice I'd made with my schooling.

"You're sorry? For what? This?"

"No. Everything. For putting so much of my problems on you. For ruining your life." His eyes welled up.

I let out a sigh as I crossed my arms. I'd never seen this side of him before. "You didn't ruin my life," I said as I walked his way. "You didn't kill Tommy. You're not responsible for Mom's death." I stopped at his laptop and pointed. "It was one of these two cowards who have been hiding all this time."

Dad hung his head, possibly trying to hide from me as best he could.

I grabbed him by the chin, something I never imagined doing to a parent, and snatched his gaze. "You want to make all of this up to me? Find us a way in to see Zach or work out how we can get the info we need from the damn US Marshal. Do whatever you have to do. Identify the girl who destroyed our family."

He nodded, firming up his expression before he wiped away his tears. "I'll do it. I won't let you down."

CHAPTER FIFTY

Marie – Now

The small revolver feels light in my hand. It looks like a snub-nose thirty-eight with no hammer. Zach taught me all about the different handguns he used in robberies. For some reason, the information stuck. There's no safety on this weapon, so I need to be careful not to touch the trigger unless I mean it. All I can hope is that tonight does not reach such a point.

"What are you doing, Marie?" Toni asks, her hands raised.

"Keep your arms down. I don't want you grabbing your dad's attention. If I see him head this way because of you, I'll shoot. Got it?"

Toni nods. She seems calmer than expected. I, on the other hand, have a surge of adrenaline running through my system that is making my hands shake a little. I need to get it together fast before she talks me into handing her the gun back. God knows it feels toxic in my hands.

"What's the plan here, Marie?" Toni pushes.

"The plan is for you to keep quiet. Now reach into your backpack and grab out a few of those damn zip tie restraints. And make sure you open the bag right up first so I can see into it."

Toni nods again. "Okay. I'll do that. There's no need to do anything—"

"Anything what? Crazy? We're past that, don't you think?" Spit comes out of my mouth as I speak. My voice cracks with emotion, but I don't care. I want this mess to be over with.

Toni keeps her hands low and wide. "It's all good. See. I'm opening the backpack. Here are the zip ties." She points into the bag.

"Take them out. Place one over your wrists." I wave the revolver.

Toni takes a moment but does as I ask her and places a plastic restraint over her hands. She can't pull the tie shut without my input. I still have a tie around my wrists and ankles, so I fish out the knife that's been sitting in my pocket all this time to awkwardly cut myself loose.

Toni's eyes light up as she sees the half-broken blade.

"You forgot about this, didn't you."

She stares at the knife. "Yes."

Fumbling a little, I slip the weapon backward into the small gap between my hands while still holding the gun. It's not an easy task, but I manage to free myself. A moment later, I work my legs loose. "Much better," I say, feeling like a fresh breeze has blown through the car.

"How could I forget the knife?" Toni asks me. "I assumed you threw it aside."

"Don't beat yourself up. We all make mistakes. Now hold out your hands." I jab the revolver at her. Toni does as she's told, the same way she did when she was pretending to be her father's captive. I carry the gun back in one hand as she turns her head from me. After a fumble, I restrain her wrists forward as tightly as possible.

"Much better. Keep up appearances. Don't let on that matters have changed to your father out there, got it?"

"Okay. No problem. And we can continue talking. There's no need for things to end badly. After all, I just wanted to chat to you and nothing more."

I shake my head, stopping myself from laughing. "You're kidding, right? All you've ever wanted from me is this damn confession, like little else in the world matters. That reminds me." I reach down to the floor of the car and retrieve the cell Toni dropped in the fight for the gun. The video is still recording everything we've been saying. I hit stop and then delete the file. Then, I go into the trash folder and destroy it for a second time before ensuring there's no cloud backup associated with the phone.

All that's left to do is to smash the phone in case someone takes it to a recovery specialist, but I'll worry about that later. I still need the device to make an important call.

Toni mutters under her breath and looks out to her distracted father.

"Hey, eyes forward. You didn't think I would forget that this thing was recording, did you?"

She chuckles to herself, half losing it. "Part of me wished you would, but I knew it was only a matter of time."

I grip the cell tight in my hand, hoping to God it has credit on it. I need to make one call, and it's not to the police. If I request the cops now without having Steven under control, he might fight the responding officers and end up in a shootout that could see me shot dead as a result. The only person I want helping me through this situation is Deputy US Marshal Dustin Taylor, and I have his number flying through my brain.

"This night has been an absolute bust," Toni says without prompting. "Hell, these last three months have been a total waste of time."

"Why? I thought you wanted to find me and make me confess everything."

"I did. When I moved in, we had eliminated our suspects down to you and one other woman. My job was to keep an eye on you while my dad watched over the other person. Do you know how hard it was for me to act like I was your friend all the while knowing you could be the one we were after? I used to stand over you while you slept, hoping that my dad would contact me that night and tell me you were Tommy's killer."

My skin crawls. "What would you have done if you found out during one of those nights?"

She glances sideways. "It's hard to say what any of us will do in any given moment."

"That's reassuring to hear."

Toni shrugs. "In the end, I found out when I was away from the house with Dad. That took us nearly three months. When I learned the truth, it almost broke me, but I pushed through it all to be here, for Tommy."

I feel the revolver falling down as Toni's honesty came through in her story. "Let me ask you something: were you always planning on drawing a confession out of me? Was that the intention from day one?"

"We never had a plan at first, but the more I learned about you, the more I wanted you to pay and be publicly shamed for getting away with his murder."

"I never got away with anything, and I didn't murder him," I say, while the gun in my hand shakes more. "I've had to live like this for five years. You of all people know how limited and pathetic my existence is."

Toni scoffs. "You think you've suffered, that your life has been hell all this time. Well, I know you enjoy your miserable world. It's clear it suits your personality down to a T."

"That's not true," I reply.

"Oh, but it is. You want to feel sorry for yourself and justify not spending a second in prison for what you did to my little brother. What better way to do that than to live like a loser."

"You don't know what you're talking about," I growl. "I am in witness protection."

"That's debatable. Yes, technically you are still in the program, but you were only under strict care for one year. Then you got transferred out here because Zach was no longer considered a major threat. He'd forgotten about you and moved on from the two people who'd put him behind bars. Maybe he even accepted his fate. But not you. No, you hung onto that romantic idea that he was obsessed with finding you. You used it to justify hiding away from the world the way you still do."

"No, I didn't. I'm not..." I say. The cell and the gun both jitter in my hand. I feel my breath quicken, but one thought keeps me going. "I was still under threat from Zach. The Deputy US Marshal assigned to my case told me to continue keeping a low profile to be safe."

"Of course he did. But he didn't tell you to hide away like a hermit and never live your life again, did he."

He didn't. But I couldn't convince myself that Zach wasn't around the corner waiting to strike. I did help to bring him down. He was never the most level-headed individual. Sure, he knew how to rob a bank with a cool steady hand, but he also would go off the handle if any of his guys questioned his methods. Why did I ever love him? What made me fall so hard for a man clearly so wrong for me in every way?

I snap out of my daydream and realize I've wasted valuable seconds talking to Toni. It won't be long until her father returns from his smoking break to find things have changed in the back seat. It's time I called Dustin. He could save me from these people and make sure they never find me again.

With one hand on the gun and the other wrapped around the cell, I do what I can to calm myself down with a few deep breaths in and out.

As I go to dial, I glance up to see Steven coming toward the car. In only a few seconds he'll be on top of me.

What the hell am I going to do?

CHAPTER FIFTY-ONE

Toni – Then

Time could be your best friend or your worst enemy depending on how you looked at it. For me, time had become a slow agonizing drain on my life. Like a vampire sucking the blood out of me drop by drop, the days dragged by. I'd work at the coffee shop, come home, and do the bare minimum to keep the house afloat. I couldn't handle much else.

A cute guy had been hitting on me at work. He'd show up there just to see me, only ordering a coffee at the most. He did his best to get me talking whenever I brought it out to him. I didn't want to hear what he had to say no matter how sweet or handsome I found him. Eventually, I gave in and went back to his house. One thing quickly led to another before we'd even had a single date. The surprise on his face was priceless, but it dropped when I told him not to contact me again. He no longer visited the coffee shop.

I didn't have the emotional availability to endure a relationship. Sure, I felt bad for the guy. He'd done nothing wrong, but I wasn't in a good place. It was easier to send him away than to wait for him to discover my numerous flaws one at a time.

I tried to help Dad wherever I could with our Zach and Dustin problem. Without being able to approach either man directly, there was little we could achieve. The only thing we could do to stay sane was to attempt to solve our problems on our own.

We needed to identify who out of Rose and Marie was the killer. Not only that, we still needed to locate them. It was like pushing an oversize boulder up a hill without knowing how much farther you had to go. We chased false leads into dead ends and worked the wrong people for information they weren't privy to. All we had to show were the girls' names and nothing more.

Time passed me by in a swirling blur. Days turned into weeks, weeks morphed into months. Almost two years evaporated before we saw our next development. Dad managed to find the two women's addresses. I preferred to remain in the dark as to how he obtained their locations, but he told me he'd found the right person with the appropriate access and paid them whatever they asked. The breakthrough was amazing but short lived as we still failed to establish who the killer was. That's when Dad came to me with an idea.

"You want me to what?"

"I want you to move in with Marie Williams. Pose as a student and keep a close eye on her."

I could feel my mouth hanging out of my jaw. "Why? You've been keeping tabs on her, right?"

"I have, but there's something about her that bothers me. I get the feeling from what I've seen that she might up and leave one day."

"And your solution to some gut instinct is for me to live with a person who may have killed my little brother?"

"I realize it's a lot to take on, but you fit the bill."

I stared at him with narrowed brows.

"She takes in students from time to time. You could pose as one. As luck would have it, she's just put up a post online to take a new one in."

I shook my head and squeezed my temples. "This is madness. You see that, right?"

"I wish there were another way," he said with genuine concern in his eyes. He wasn't messing around.

"And what about Rose Melton?"

"I'll continue to monitor her. She doesn't strike me as the sort who's looking to leave."

I exhaled, feeling the air flow over the two palms gripping my face. "Fine. But only for Mom and Tommy."

"Thank you," Dad whispered as he pulled me in for a hug.

"Just promise me something," I said. "As soon as you realize who did it between Rose and Marie, you wait until I'm away from her before you tell me. If I find out it was Marie when I'm with her, I don't know what I'll do."

He stared at me without judgment. We both had no idea what we'd do if we ever came face to face with the killer. "I promise."

CHAPTER FIFTY-TWO

I thought about the only two people in the world who could tell dad and me who shot Tommy: Deputy US Marshal Dustin Taylor and Zachary Sanchez.

Dustin was fast becoming our best hope of finding the truth when we got rejected for the third time in a row to visit Zach. Despite using false names, he refused to let anyone come and see him. The prison had done something to his mind. The Marshal became the only person we had left.

Whether he knew it, the man was a barrier between us and everything we wanted. None of Dad's research ever indicated the guilty one. Whenever it seemed like we had a solid lead, the trail fizzled out. Short of bribing Dustin, we'd hit a brick wall all the while knowing we could never climb it.

I moved in with Marie. Dad seemed to focus less and less on the two girls. While I had to live with the potential enemy, he gave me fewer updates and even talked about returning to work. I couldn't discourage him from doing so, but I also didn't want him to forget about Tommy or Mom. Especially while I was down in Arizona side by side with 'Karen'. We were so close to the end.

"What are we going to do?" I asked him when I was home one day taking a few days off from watching Marie. We were sitting in traffic on our way to Walmart. It was apparent that we might never learn the truth.

"What can we do?" Dad asked. "We've exhausted every other avenue, and Zach is a no go. Maybe it's time we moved on from all of this and got you back home for good, you know."

My mouth fell open. I couldn't believe what he was suggesting. "Are you serious? You're saying we should cut our losses? That I shouldn't continue to live with Marie?"

He gave me a shrug. "Well, yeah. We've wasted too many hours on nothing. I've ruined my career and need to retrain if I ever want to be an EMT again. You've spoiled your chances at finishing college. What will they make you do before you can retake your course? It was crazy for me to put you down in Arizona with one of the girls."

"I don't care about any of that. Besides, I have the rest of my life to finish school."

"I can't have you wasting more of your time only to work back to where you were when this all began."

"That's my problem. Plus, I chose to do this. I wanted to come home and help the family. I made the effort to live with Marie like you asked me to."

Dad shook his head. "I know that, and I appreciate everything you've sacrificed for me, but you should be thinking of your future instead. It's the way things are supposed to be done."

"No, Dad. You were right to put all of your focus on this. Tommy's death can't be shoved aside and ignored. His killer needs to pay for what she did. Mom deserves for her pain and suffering to have meant something."

Dad fell silent for a minute and stared out his window away from the traffic ahead. There'd been a car accident outside the giant parking lot holding us up.

"What is it?" I asked him. I never liked it when he went quiet on me.

"Nothing."

"Come on. You can't do that. Tell me."

He sighed with closed eyes. "I shouldn't say anything, but it's about your mother."

"What about her?" My heart skipped a beat.

"It's more about what she did," he said, turning back to me.

My pupils darted in my head as I attempted to understand what he was getting at.

"How she died," he said.

"What about it?" I sat up straight.

"I wish I had said this to you at the time, but what she did was wrong. She shouldn't have tried to solve her problems with drugs and alcohol. Sure, we weren't there for her the way we should have been, but it didn't give her the right to choose that path. She knew better."

My hands reached for my temples. "I don't know how to respond, Dad."

"You don't have to say a word."

"Maybe I should though. Maybe it was the appropriate choice for her to make."

Dad gripped the steering wheel tight. "No, it wasn't, okay? It was the easy thing to do."

I pressed myself sideways against the door. "How can you think that? She was suffering. She was in agony in a dark place with no one there to pull her out. It was the only way she could cope."

"We're all in pain over what happened to Tommy. Every single day I'm reminded that some pathetic loser shot and killed my son. But you don't see me drinking myself to death, do you?"

I remained silent and allowed his words to hang in the air, unanswered. He didn't drink himself to death or take a fistful of pills each day, but his pain had transformed him in other ways.

Dad continued. "You understand what I mean, right? You may never want to hear about it, but it happened. And now we're left behind to deal with it all. I've spent my time trying to get justice for Tommy, and it's taken a toll on my wellbeing."

"Have you given up?" I asked, keeping my eyes locked onto his.

"Not given up. I'm just coming to the end of it all. There's a light out there in our dark world, and I want to find it."

I wanted to ask him something more, but the words never came out. Instead, I tried to understand what he was saying. Was he right? I couldn't allow myself to think he was correct in any capacity. My mother was suffering. She was hurt. I always felt now she didn't have to deal with the torment of living each day with a dead son in her wake, but really, it was naïve of me to believe.

I faced my dad again and asked him a question I never hoped would come out of my mouth. "Should we give up?"

He drove the car forward as the traffic eased. He turned to me with a shrug. "Maybe it's time. Maybe the best thing we can do for Tommy and your mom is to just move on with our lives."

I felt the sting of tears filling my eyes as a lump in my throat formed. The pain held me frozen in place and stopped me from responding. How could we ever consider giving up? Would anyone else do so if someone murdered their little brother? Would they let their mother's overdose equate to nothing? I tried to speak, but all I managed to do was cough and cry at the same time.

"Are you okay?" Dad asked me as we reached the Walmart parking lot. He pulled into the nearest space he could find despite it being almost a few hundred yards from the entrance.

As soon as we stopped, it all came out. I burst into tears and threw both hands over my face. Dad grabbed hold of me and yanked me toward him.

"It's okay, honey. Let it out. Just let it out." He patted my back and tried to soothe me like I was a little kid who'd fallen off their bike and scraped a knee. I felt warm and safe in his arms, something I hadn't experienced in too long a time.

Once I settled down, I thought about what he'd said about quitting. There was still one thing weighing on my mind. One leaf left unturned: Dustin Taylor. I couldn't consciously let this all go without going down that avenue.

I explained myself to Dad as best I could. He nodded and remained quiet. I could tell this was an issue he was hoping to avoid. "Well?" I asked.

"Okay. I'll call him tomorrow and ask to meet somewhere at least. If he won't agree to that, I'll throw it all out there and pray for a good result."

"Thank you. If this doesn't work, I'll come back home, and we can give up."

CHAPTER FIFTY-THREE

Marie – Now

Steven reaches the car on Toni's side and sees her wrists bound with a zip tie. By the time his eyes find me on the opposite seat, I have the revolver aimed at his heart through the rear window.

"Don't move!" I yell loud enough for him to hear. "Arms up."

He stares at me for a few seconds with a snarl at the edge of his lips that is dying to come out. His fists slowly rise.

"Put them on the back of your head and interlace your fingers." I have no idea if this is what I should do to keep him at bay. I'm only doing what I've seen actors do on police dramas.

"Good. Now don't move," I say as I remove one of my trembling hands from the gun to open the door behind me. I pat around until I find the handle and give it a quick pull. The door remains shut. I try it again and a third time only to remember the child-lock feature is engaged. "Crap," I mutter. How could I forget?

Steven smiles down at me with both palms on his head. "Something the matter?" he asks, knowing exactly what my problem is.

"Don't move or talk." I place my spare hand back on the revolver to give myself a moment to think. He is armed and is seconds away from running or shooting. I need to get him under control before it's too late.

"Is this really the best idea?" he asks with a shrug.

"Shut your mouth!" Spit hangs off the end of my lips. He knows how to push my buttons. I have to pull my emotions into line, so I draw my eyes from his for a few seconds to think. "Okay, I want you to take out your gun and slowly place it on the trunk of the car. Understand?"

His gaze narrows in for a moment. Giving up his weapon is the last thing this guy enjoys doing. I'm on the right path.

Steven does as he's told and places his pistol on the lid of the trunk. He even slides it toward me for added measure.

"Good," I say. "Now, very slowly, move around to my door and open it. Don't try anything funny."

He rolls his eyes and shakes his head with a mutter, but he complies by shuffling to my side of the car. When Steven reaches the end of the vehicle, I realize he has to pass by the rear pillar. For a moment, I won't be able to see him. Has he noticed the same thing?

"Slower," I say.

But it doesn't help. His eyes flick to the blind spot and see the only opportunity he'll have to escape. He drops behind the blind spot out of sight and rushes around the SUV. I have no idea where he is.

"No, no, no," I mutter as I try to turn in multiple directions at once in the limited space of the back seat to locate him. One second, I feel the vehicle shake from the front, but by the time I've turned a rattle happens on the other side. He's messing with me, spinning me in circles to make me as confused as possible so he can reclaim his weapon from the hood of the trunk.

Like an idiot, I try the door handle again as if the child lock has somehow stopped working. It doesn't budge, not even when I slam my fist on it several times. I need the damn car to open, and it occurs to me now that there's only one way out. My idea is insane, but it reminds me I'm holding a spare set of keys to the outside world in my palms: the revolver.

Closing both eyes and blocking an ear, I fire the gun at the glass of my door. Expecting it to blast all over my face, I'm surprised to see the window crumble mostly outward. The pane must be made of safety glass as none of the pieces are sharp when I stretch my arm out the opening to the exterior handle. Within a second, the door opens, and I stumble out, half losing my footing as I sweep my head around the street looking for Steven. I reach into my pocket. In one palm, I hold the cell phone that was recording me. In the other, the revolver. I'm ready to do what I have to do to survive, but I don't see him anywhere.

"Where are you?" I call out. He doesn't respond, so I move my way down to the trunk. If I can get my hands on his pistol, I'll be safe. Relief washes over me when I spot it still in place. His game of cat and mouse went on for too long. I no doubt spooked him when I blasted out the glass, forcing him to retreat a little.

I charge at the second weapon only to see a hand slide up and over the other side of the car to retrieve it. Steven's head pops up a fraction later to extend his reach.

"Stop," I yell, pointing my pistol at his skull. He freezes on the spot with his fingers less than a foot away from his gun.

"I'm not playing. If you touch that thing, I'll shoot." I keep my aim as steady as possible while Steven's eyes remain fixed on the weapon. He craves it more than anything else in the world, all because he wishes to see me dead.

We hold this standoff pose for at least ten seconds before a silence takes over. I can hear only the ambiance of the night over the sound of our ragged breathing. I do what I can to keep my focus as images from the past try to flash through my brain. I have to shrug them away if I have half a chance of keeping Steven under control.

I think about the gunshot and wonder if someone has called the police. What will happen if they find us like this? How do I explain everything before an officer shoots me, assuming I'm the bad guy?

"Got ourselves a situation here," Steven says.

"Yes, we do," I reply.

He edges his arm back and places it on the car to rest. I study his face for a few seconds. Neither of us knows what to do, and we're doing a lousy job of hiding it.

"Your move," he says.

CHAPTER FIFTY-FOUR

Toni – Then

D ad made the call in front of me the next day as promised. To my amazement, Dustin agreed to meet with him later, saying he was in the area. Naturally, I begged to come along.

"Please, Dad. I have to. This is too important for me not to be there," I said as we sat around the dining room table.

"But he's only expecting to see me. He knows who I am and my history. He doesn't know what I want, either. If he sees you there too, he might suspect we're up to something."

We still weren't clear on what it was we would do when we identified Tommy's killer. All we were concerned about was the hunt. I answered him back with the best idea I had. "If he asks why I'm there, it's to support you. Just be as sad as you can when you talk, and he'll get it." It wasn't far from the truth. We were both miserable people, even on a good day.

Dad pursed his lips to think about it for a moment. "Fine. Come along, but don't say a single word other than 'hello' or 'goodbye' to the man. We can't let on that you're living with Marie or that we're here to find out which of the two killed Tommy. One wrong move and he might call it in and have us arrested or have them moved."

"Arrested for what? Finding out who escaped justice for shooting a child, of all things. Why does that person deserve protection?"

Dad didn't answer me. There was no need to speak about something we both wished wasn't the truth. He twirled his cell on the table, possibly to distract himself.

I tried to think of a way to calm myself down and not have another outburst again in front of him, but a question brimmed at the edge of my mind. "So, how do we get Dustin Taylor to tell us what we want? After all, we only need to know who."

"My plan is simple. How well it works depends on Taylor."

"Okay?"

"Once I get a feel for what he's like and what he thinks of the whole thing, I'll urge him to spill who did it between the two girls. I'll advise him that our conversation never happened, and that we didn't get the information from him. If he wants cash, I've got ten thousand dollars good to go."

I felt my mouth fall half open. "That's the grand plan? Just beg for the truth and throw money in his face? Come on, Dad. That won't work. He's a US Marshal. He'll arrest you, possibly me as well."

Dad stood from the dining chair, making the seat squeak. "What else am I supposed to do, huh? Point a gun at him and force the truth out?"

"Obviously not. That's why we need to think this through. He's agreed to speak with you. That's got to mean something, right? Maybe we be indirect with our questioning."

"What? Be subtle? How can that work? We want to find Tommy's killer and bring her to justice. No amount of bullshit will make this guy believe we're after anything else."

I had nothing to say and gave him a shrug. He hated my response and stormed off on me. I didn't stop him. We both needed time alone to calm down.

***

The next day, I came out to the kitchen to find Dad all set to go. We only had to drive a short distance to Denver where Dustin was staying in a hotel. He agreed to meet Dad at the bar around lunchtime. I didn't know if that was a good thing or not. All I could hope for was that Mr. Taylor would have loose lips when we arrived.

"You ready?" Dad asked me.

"Yep. Have been for hours," I replied. I wasn't sure if he'd still invite me after our heated discussion the day before.

"Then let's get this over with."

We both headed out, taking Dad's car the short twenty-minute trip to Denver. I almost wished it was further for us to go for the meeting. It would give me more time to think. I could never see things for what they were when I was stuck at home. The open road was the best place for my mind to process the many thoughts in my head, and I never got to drive anywhere these days.

Before I knew it, we were there, parked out front of a small Denver hotel, early, to visit a Deputy US Marshal to find out who killed our Tommy.

We walked into the daunting foyer of the resort together and headed for the bar. Dad moved ahead of me, so his face would be the first thing Dustin saw.

We located him in a booth all alone, knowing what he looked like from a photo found online. He spotted the two of us and didn't look surprised. Instead, he waved us over as if we all knew each other from way back when.

"Hello, Steven," Dustin said once we were close enough. "And this must be Toni. How are you doing, dear?"

I went to answer, but he cut me off.

"Dumb question. Forget I asked it. Take a seat, the both of you."

We gave each other a quick glance when it became apparent Dustin had been drinking. The half-empty beer he had his hand around couldn't be the first one he'd tossed back that day.

I waited for Dad to sit on the opposite side of the booth and sat in beside him. I felt so insignificant being there, like a little kid who'd tagged along with her father. What was I thinking?

"So, what brings the two remaining Prices to me?" Dustin asked, not wasting anyone's time.

"Well, sir, you obviously know our history. You can appreciate what we've been through."

"I do."

"I guess, what moves us to meet with you today is not an easy thing to go over. And frankly, it's a problem that's been on our minds since Tommy got shot."

Dustin huffed. "Is that so?" he asked before he drank the other half of his beer. He raised his hand to order another drink. "Out with it. What do you need to know?"

Dad looked to me. We peered at each other for a moment, silently communicating to go ahead as one, but Dad stood, trying to spare me from any wrongdoing.

"I want you to tell me who shot Tommy. I believe it's either Rose Melton or Marie Williams."

Dustin didn't move an inch. He glared at Dad until his beer came. It got placed on the table in the middle of stone-cold silence. "Are you serious?" Dustin asked.

Dad took in a deep breath and let it all out before answering. "Yes, I am. I know one of them shot my little boy and caused my wife's downward spiral. It's been so long without a whiff of justice for these people you protect. All I want to learn is who broke my family apart. No one ever needs to find out who told me. You get me?"

Dustin grabbed his open beer and took a decent swig. He exhaled a satisfied lungful of the beverage and spun toward me. "And what about you, young Antoinette?" he asks using the long version of my first name. "Do you demand vengeance for your baby brother and mother?"

I didn't know what to say. I twisted to Dad, but Dustin grabbed the hand of mine that was resting on the table. "Don't look to him for answers. Tell me what you want to happen."

What do I want to happen? My wants became irrelevant so long ago I'd almost forgotten them. Now it was only the things we needed that drove me forward, that gave me a reason to get up in the morning and keep going. But I didn't know that then.

I tried to speak, but the lump in my throat returned, not letting a single word out.

CHAPTER FIFTY-FIVE

Marie – Now

How did it come to this? I never pictured being in such a situation again after spending five years trying to escape such a dark world. But here I am, aiming a handgun at another human being.

I'll never forget that moment when I shot Tommy Price. I see it on repeat in my head whenever I'm around a gun of any sort. Holding one in my hand is like trying to hold a lit torch the wrong way up. My every instinct wants me to throw the thing into a river.

I stare at Steven as he stares at his pistol on the trunk of his car. I have him dead to rights and could blast him away in an instant. But I know, deep down, that I won't be able to pull this trigger. I can't after last time.

Steven sighs, shifting his eyes from the gun to mine. His shoulders relax a little. "I'm going to reach into my pocket and take out a pack of smokes and a lighter. Is that okay?"

"Fine. Just do it as slowly as you can."

"I will," he says. "But I can see you have your finger wrapped around the trigger. Please remove it. I'm not looking to get shot anytime soon."

Glancing down at the revolver in my hand, I realize what he is saying. I quickly withdraw my finger from the trigger and place it along the guard for safety.

Steven flicks his lighter as he shoves a stick into his mouth. On the third try, he is successful. The cigarette sparks bright through the flame, piercing the dark night. As he exhales a cloud of smoke,

I look at Toni in the SUV. She's been watching us the whole time, waiting to see who will come out on top of this hell.

"Get out of the car," I call to Toni. "And bring the zip ties from your bag."

"What you got planned there?" Steven asks, jutting the cigarette in my direction.

"Never you mind," I say, trying to ignore him.

"The thing is, I do mind, Marie. And I'll give you until I finish my smoke here to tell me before I make things interesting for us all."

I tighten the aim I have on him. I don't know what he is thinking dishing out orders to me. Surely he won't reach for the gun on the trunk? Has he worked out my bluff? My squaring up doesn't seem to bother him as much as it should.

Toni breaks the tension a little when she reaches Steven's side with the zip ties. She only has the one on around her wrists. There's nothing stopping her from running except me and this revolver. I stare at her wondering if she knows I won't shoot if push comes to shove. Sweat drips from my brow.

I refocus on Steven and see his cigarette is almost finished. Without taking my eyes off him, I give his daughter an order that may cause this situation to explode. "Toni. Please put a zip tie on your father's wrists and pull the strap tight."

A grave look washes over Toni's face. She holds the restraint out in her hands but doesn't move.

"You can do this. He's not going to do anything stupid. He'll do what I tell him, won't you, Steven?"

I get no response. Instead, he lifts his cigarette in the air to draw in the last breath of smoke the stick has left in it. Just as his fingers reach his mouth, he stops with a grin.

"What are you planning to do once we're all tied up, huh? You can't handle the both of us and carry that thing."

He has a point, but it's one I've already thought of. I hold out the cell phone Toni tried to use before to get a confession out of me.

Steven's eyes go wide.

Did he not notice the device in my hand? "I've got a call to make."

"What? To the cops? How do you explain all this to them? You'd lose control of the situation fast. They'd shoot first and ask questions later."

"Never said I was calling the police. You shouldn't assume so much." I dial a number I have committed to memory. One I always had at the forefront of my mind anytime I feared for my life in this whole witness protection thing. Dustin's cell was available twenty-four-seven. He told me he'd answer it no matter what. It's time to test his words.

"Who are you calling?" Steven demands.

I am a single digit away from dialing out and connecting with Dustin. I stop with my finger hovering over the final number as I look up.

"Well?" Steven presses.

"If you must know, I'm about to call the Deputy US Marshal assigned to my case."

His eyes flick around. "Him? Ha, that's a waste of time."

"Why?" I ask, keeping my gaze locked onto his. Something about this has got him rattled. I get the overwhelming feeling I need to find out.

Steven draws the final portion of smoke from his cigarette and blows it out into the night. He drops the butt and stomps it flat.

I don't look away. He's trying to make me falter and stumble, but I can see it in his eyes. Dustin is the last person he'd ever want me to talk to. He knows the US Marshal will save me from him and his daughter.

"We'll see," I say as I go to press the button.

"You don't understand," Toni interrupts.

I shift my aim to her without thinking. "Understand what? You're both trying to mess with me. That's all you've done since you showed up on my doorstep. I'm calling Dustin and that's that."

Steven makes his move and snatches the gun from the trunk. The world around me slows down as I turn the revolver toward him. But he is too fast. Our aims meet in the middle as one. We both have our weapons locked in on each other's head, fingers on triggers, ready to end the discussion.

CHAPTER FIFTY-SIX

I can't hear a thing. Not the slight breeze rolling in from the desert. Not the city in the distance. Not even the sound of my staggered breathing. I focus my senses on Steven pointing his pistol on me, ready to fire, as I do the same to him.

Neither of us says a word, letting our weapons do the talking. We both have clear shots of one another and are waiting for someone to squeeze off a single round to resolve the night.

"Wait," Toni says, butting in on our discussion of sorts. "No one shoot. It doesn't have to end this way."

"It's obvious this is what she wants!" Steven yells. "Just get out of here."

"I'm not going anywhere," Toni says.

There's no fear in her voice. Her words don't wobble and crack the way mine would if I could utter a single sound right now.

"Dammit, Toni. Listen to me. This is between the two of us. Take my keys and go before anything happens."

"No. I'm not losing you as well. Hasn't she taken enough from our family?"

I won't to respond, but I can't shift my eyes from Steven to Toni. If I even blink for more than a split second, he will kill me.

"It won't come to that, will it Marie?" Steven asks.

I don't answer straight away, trying to determine how serious he is. "What are you getting at?"

"I'm not getting at anything. I just think we both need to put our guns down before either of us does something we regret. Wouldn't you agree?"

I dart my eyes left and right between each of his pupils trying to discern what he's up to. This has to be a trick. I have to remember the lies these two have fed me from the start. I know in my heart I can't trust a word that comes out either of their mouths, so I say nothing.

"Come on," Toni says. "Is this what you want?"

Her words draw me into a memory as I think about the question when it was posed to me almost five years ago.

I was sitting inside an interrogation room, having spent the last ten-plus hours being grilled by two detectives over the gas station shooting and robbery. One of the men stood over me from the side while the other sat across from me on the table.

"Is this what you want?" the one standing over me asked, his breath heavy with coffee.

It was a dumb question. Who would hope to find themselves about to go to prison for ever after, having accidentally shot a boy during a robbery gone wrong?

"Just tell us everything you know about Zachary Sanchez and we can talk about a deal. Maybe get your jail time cut down to something more reasonable."

I shook my head, unable to process the information being thrown at me. I'd foolishly waived my right to have a lawyer present, not being able to think straight when asked the question. They wanted me to give up everything I knew about Zach. How could I do such a thing?

We were both arrested when the police found us hiding away in a cheap motel room. A team of heavily armed police came crashing into our room and had us both restrained on the ground in less than a minute. The detectives strolled in once the dust had settled and read us our rights. The next thing I realized, we'd been hauled in to a police station and got separated into different interrogation rooms.

"You obviously know him well. Tell me what kind of person he is," the detective across from me pressed.

I focused all my efforts on not revealing the list of terrible things I knew about Zach. He tried to save me from getting arrested and gave me money to flee. But I couldn't leave his side and begged him to help me. We were headed for the border into Mexico, but never made it that far. I don't know how, but the police tracked us down.

"He's not messing around here," the other man said. Their faces were a partial blur in my memory. I wasn't all there in that moment. Shock had set in and taken hold of my ability to think straight.

"Right now, we've got you for attempted murder, fleeing the scene of a crime, attempted armed robbery, and whatever else we can dream up to throw at you. You'll be lucky to see the light of day after we're done."

"Unless," the first detective says, drawing out the word to grab my attention. "Unless you tell us what we want to hear. Tell us about Zach. We can see he pulled you out of the gas station. Tell me why a career criminal would risk putting his face on camera just to save someone like you?" His finger tapped on the glass of a laptop screen, showing me CCTV footage of my blundered robbery. It was a surreal moment.

I tried to speak, to say anything to shut out the two men in suits, but the door to the interrogation room burst open. My head snapped to the precinct outside of the ever-shrinking space to see yet another man in a suit enter. Was this a third officer sent in to break me?

The man flashed his credentials. "Deputy US Marshal Dustin Taylor. I'll be taking over this case from here."

One man rose from the square table faster than I'd seen him move all day. "Bullshit. This is our case. You can't just come in here and—"

The second detective grabbed his partner and pulled him back. "Ease down. Let's not get ahead of ourselves. Can I see your paperwork, Deputy?"

"It's all here," Dustin said handing over a fistful of documents while he kept his eyes locked onto mine.

We all waited as the detective read through the file. He shook his head several times until his shoulders dropped. "You can't be serious?"

"Afraid so. Now if you fellas don't mind, I'd like you to shut off that recording and leave the room."

The two detectives complied with mutters under their breaths along with a few choice cuss words. Within a minute, they were gone as if the long day we'd spent together never happened.

Dustin sat down opposite me and dumped his wad of files on the metal table. He methodically pulled out printouts of the CCTV footage showing a grainy close-up of Zach.

"What's this? I already told the other two all I will say about Zach."

"I don't think you did. And the problem comes down to my colleagues out there not asking you the right questions."

I scrunched my brow. "What is that supposed to mean?"

"It's simple. I'm here with a different kind of offer. One you can't refuse."

And he was right. It was too good a deal to walk away from. Dustin was like a guardian angel who appeared from nowhere to save me from a life of hell on the inside. I only wish I had the courage back then to decline his offer to testify against Zach. I wouldn't have been here now facing off with the father of the boy I'd shot.

"Well? Is this what you want?" Toni asks again. "Is this the answer?"

Her desperate question pulls me back into the present. I let my eyes shift to Toni's while my pistol stays locked onto Steven. She sees me and asks her question again by leaning toward me with her hands outstretched. "Well?"

"Of course this isn't what I wanted. No one ever would..." I feel myself trail off, unable to finish my thought. The arm holding my weapon up shakes, itching to be lower down.

"Then why don't you both put the guns away at the same time? No one else needs to die, do they."

I try to gauge Steven's reaction as Toni's unanswered question hangs in the air between us all. He doesn't lower his weapon and neither do I.

"Please. It doesn't have to be this way," she calls out. "We can work this out. Dad?"

Steven's eyes dart toward his daughter. He stares at her for too long and lets out an audible huff into the night. His arm sinks. I follow suit, matching his slow speed.

Toni doesn't hide her delight as we both hang our pistols at our sides. "Thank you. This is the right thing to do. We can talk this out."

I keep the pistol out. Steven does the same. Toni might be ready to declare peace between us, but we don't trust each other. How can we? The only thing we all do well is lie to one another.

"Now what?" Steven asks his daughter.

"We talk."

"Talk?" he asks.

"I'm serious. We talk it out. No threats."

"And then what? Part ways? Forget the whole thing?"

Toni takes in a deep breath. It's clear she's wrestling with some heavy thoughts. "Maybe it's for the best. Maybe we should never have come here."

He shakes his head, ready to argue, but Toni places her hand on his wrist before he raises his pistol back up. He relaxes his shoulders, but I can still feel his hatred beaming out for me.

"This isn't what any of us want, is it, Marie," Toni says.

I stare at her while Steven looks away defeated. I'm safe for now, only because she's around to keep him at bay. But what happens when she can no longer keep him under control? "This isn't what I wanted," I say, holding her gaze. "But maybe it's what needs to happen." I raise my pistol at Steven. Neither of them has time to react as I close my eyes and squeeze the trigger.

The gun in my hand rings out a bullet into the night.

CHAPTER FIFTY-SEVEN

I never wanted things to go this way, but the past I tried so hard to hide away from is determined to make me pay for my mistakes. Steven Price will never stop pursuing me until I've suffered as much as humanly possible. What choice did I have but to put a stop to him?

The smoking revolver hangs limp in my hand as I hold my eyes shut. I don't want to open them and face reality, but I need to see what I've done. When I take a peek, I see a bewildered Steven staring at me, eyes wide. I missed.

The gun lowers when I realize I tried to kill him. How could I have considered such a thing? The revolver falls free from my fingers into gravity's control. My hands and body shake as I back away from a frozen Steven and Toni.

"I didn't mean to..." I utter, unsure what I'm saying. But my legs take over and turn me around. I run. Away from them both. Away from the pistol before I do something else.

"Stop!" Steven yells. "Come back here."

I can't stop though. I don't know where I'm going, but no amount of words will slow me down.

Reaching the other side of the road, I cut through an open lot. Dust and rocks kick up with every stride taken as I glance over my shoulder to see Steven charge after me. Toni isn't far behind.

I have no clue where to run to, but I have one move left to play. The cell stays clutched in my grip. I managed to hold on to it while the revolver fell out of my hand. The phone is more valuable given who I can make a call to.

Dustin's number runs through my mind, each digit cemented in my long-term memory. I've waited all night to place this call.

The US Marshal is the only person who can save me from this father-daughter duo.

Steven yells out again as I reenter Dustin's cell number into the phone. I stumble before the last two digits spill out of my brain and into the device. My legs keep me upright, stopping me from kissing the gravel.

"Marie!" Steven yells.

He's gaining on me. I focus on what I need to do and finish dialing. As I tap the call button, I pick up the pace to put some distance between us.

I cross out from the empty lot into the next road as the cell connects and rings. I take another peek back as I bring the phone to my ear to see Toni rocket past her father.

Her legs pump harder than mine ever could as she barrels down on me. If I don't lose her somehow, I'll never be able to talk with Dustin and escape this hell.

I spot a narrow lane and charge toward it. But instead of running down the straight pathway where Toni can catch me, I jump a fence into someone's backyard.

Landing with a thud, I continue on and hear Dustin's cell ring out to an answering service. "Dammit!" I yell, loud enough to wake an oversize American Pit Bull Terrier. The alert beast, bares its teeth, stopping me where I stand. Toni doesn't follow over the barricade.

With no other choice, I run for a nearby gate as fast as I can. The upset animal follows quicker than Toni and barks at me. I bash through the chain-link door and slam it shut as the dog crashes into the rusty metal. Fangs and spit snap out toward my face as I use my full body to hold the door closed.

An angry voice yells out to the backyard from the occupant of the house, causing Toni and Steven to back away before they receive the blame for creating a disturbance.

"Shut the hell up, Daisy," the man yells. "Get your butt over here."

The dog, conflicted, snaps its attention between me and its master. I don't make a sound or move a muscle, praying the dog obeys its owner.

With a low growl followed by a whimper, Daisy gives in to the command and leaves me at the gate. I let out a thankful sigh and close my eyes for a moment. When I open them, I turn away, focus ahead, and run.

I rush out the front of the person's property I had just trespassed on and scan the area left and right. Toni and Steven are nowhere to be found, so I sprint along the road. The headlights from a car in the distance grab my attention. Fortunately, the vehicle turns away before it reaches me. I let out a sigh of relief and duck behind a half wall that separates the residential properties with an industrial section.

With a slight feeling of safety in my hands, I redial Dustin. His cell rings again, telling me his device is at least on. "Come on, come on. Pick up the phone. You promised you'd always be there for me. No matter what."

Voicemail again. I contemplate leaving a message but Toni's voice in the distance silences me and urges me to creep further down and elsewhere from the road. If they spot me now, I'm done for. I've all but used up my energy.

I press my body as hard as I can into the wall while squatting low with my breath held. Toni and Steven sail past without seeing me hiding there. I exhale the second they're far enough away and slide down to the ground. I have to get a hold of Dustin. If he doesn't answer this time, I'll have no choice but to call the police instead.

My finger taps the button again and to redial Dustin's number. It rings as before. One ring. Two rings. "Come on." Three rings. Four rings. "Pick up, pick up, pick up." Five rings. Six. I'm ready to give up when he finally answers.

"Hello?"

I try to talk, but I'm unsure why Dustin didn't answer with a more official string of words. My throat closes up, wondering if I've called the wrong number. Could I have misremembered it?

"Hello? Who's this? I can hear you there."

"Dustin," I blurt out, knowing his voice. Relief washes over me as I realize I'm one step closer to being saved. "It's Marie. Marie Williams. I need your help, right now."

Silence meets my words as I back up further down the wall. The structure transitions into a lane that connects out to a road at the other side. I wait in agony for Dustin to respond on the other end. "Dustin? Are you there?" I'm aware of the desperation in my voice. I don't care though. I need him now more than ever.

"I'm here, Marie."

"Oh, thank God. You have to help me. Tommy Price. His family has found me. They kidnapped me and held me hostage for hours, making me confess to the whole thing. They've gone crazy. Please I'm—"

"Marie," he says.

I freeze with uncertainty.

"Slow down. Tell me everything."

I nod despite him not being able to see me. "Okay. I'll start from the beginning..." And I do. I pace around the lane, feeling the world spin into some level of order as I fill him in on the brief version of my hell. "They infiltrated my home. They knew it all. Who I was, my real name, my weaknesses. God, even things I only shared with Zach." I stop pacing when I realize I'm at the end of the lane near a patch of road again.

"Where are you now?" Dustin asks.

"Somewhere close to an industrial zone outside the city. I got away, but they're sweeping through the streets to locate me. I need your help, please. What should I do?"

Dustin doesn't answer. He instead breathes down the line. "There's only one thing you can do."

"What is it? Tell me. I'll do anything."

"Let them find you, Marie."

"What?"

"You heard me. I said let them find you."

"Why would I do that? Do you know something?"

"Do I know something?" he asks with a snicker in his voice. "I know who you are, Marie. I know what you did to their little boy, and it's pained me for five years to think I had to protect you of all people just to put some piece of shit criminal away for life who would have eventually ended up inside at some point."

"No," I utter, feeling the blood drain from my face. "You—"

"Yes, Marie. I told the Prices everything. They know who you are. They came to me having learned it was either you or Rose Melton who had killed their Tommy. Something snapped when I stared into their eyes. I don't know what it was, but I could no longer protect someone who didn't deserve to be alive while the remains of a family suffered."

I stumble backward and feel the edge of the road. "You swore you'd never betray me. You're a US Marshal."

"Not anymore. I'd already given my notice when the Prices made contact. I'm retiring early. No longer will I have to keep scum like you safe, Marie."

"You son of a bitch!" I yell. "You've killed me."

"You did that yourself the second you tried to enter a world you didn't belong in. So long, Marie." The phone disconnects.

"No!" I yell. "You bastard." My words blare out into the night with an echo. I throw the cell as hard as I can in a random direction. It smashes over the road with a crunch. A moment later, I see Toni and Steven at the end of the lane running straight at me.

"Screw you!" I yell. "I'm right here. Come get—"

My legs lift from underneath me as the world turns upside down. A blinding white flash strikes the side of my head and twists my vision in half until nothing but the dark is all I can fathom.

I see a set of blue eyes stare at me from the void.

CHAPTER FIFTY-EIGHT

Toni

The car came out of nowhere. I've never seen a person run down in the street like that before. Dad and I stand breathless and stunned over a hundred feet from where Marie's body landed. She's lying still behind an idling sedan. Smoke from its exhaust melds with the glow of red brake lights.

The driver spots us staring at the scene and hits the gas. Tires squeal as rubber and asphalt fight each other. The car speeds off into the night as the driver commits to a choice they will have to grapple with for the rest of their life.

I don't say a word to Dad as my legs take me over to Marie on the ground. He follows behind as we both approach her. She stirs and writhes around slightly, trying to understand what has happened. Her arms attempt to lift her back to her feet, but the energy has been sapped from every muscle in her body.

I come to a stop at a small pool of blood and can see one of her legs is bleeding like a tap. From my basic medical understanding of the situation, it appears the car has severed her femoral artery. She'll be dead within a minute if we don't do something.

Dad drops to a squat on autopilot. He pulls the knife out from his belt and cuts part of his dress shirt off to make a tourniquet to stem the bleeding. His EMT instincts have kicked in despite the history he and the patient have.

As he rips the piece of cloth into a long enough bit of material, my hand leans out and lands on his wrist. Our eyes come together.

I see Tommy in Dad every second I am forced to stare into his blue eyes.

I think back to the last day I saw my brother alive. I was visiting home over the break and was more interested in seeing old friends from town than having anything to do with my young sibling. All he wanted to do was spend a few hours with me and show me what new toys he had been playing with or the drawings he'd done at school.

What was I doing in those moments? I was scattered and concerned only with what I would have to wear for a catch-up with some classmates I was slowly falling out with. They didn't care about me the way Tommy did. But that didn't stop me from taking him for granted. Now, I have to live with the image of his disappointed face for the rest of my life.

Tears fill my eyes and heart as Dad shows he understands why I'm touching his wrist.

"Are you sure?" he asks me, both hands ready in case I change my mind.

I nod, unable to speak.

"Okay," he says as he puts the cloth into his pocket. He stands up and walks away, no doubt having seen enough people hurt this way in his life.

I stay squatted down as Marie half rolls over to face me. Her fading eyes find mine in the dark and plead. Does she understand what's happening? Can she see her end is coming?

I watch as it happens, as the fight drains from her soul one second at a time. With her last burst of energy, her arm reaches out to me. I don't know if it is to beg or to stop me from watching her. Either way, I hold her hand and forever seal this moment away inside my mind.

Her head drops to the asphalt with a thud as she stares up at nothing. She's gone. I have finally brought Tommy's killer to justice. Death will stop her from ever harming another human being.

I wait for the change to happen, for the moment I've been desperate to see arrive. It has given Marie what she deserves, but my mind isn't purged of every emotion this week has thrown at me. I don't feel a sense of righteous joy overwhelm me with the knowledge she is dead.

"Come on," Dad says as he grips my shoulder. "It's time to go."

I rise to my feet and take in the choice I have made.

CHAPTER FIFTY-NINE

Marie is dead. Officially, she died from a hit-and-run driver carelessly texting on his phone when she stepped out into the road. The man came forward a few hours later to see if the person he'd struck was still alive. The police arrested him straight away when he admitted the truth in an open and shut case.

I finish reading the news report on my phone in our hotel room, exhausted from the night we'd spent trying to encourage Marie to re-confess to shooting Tommy. Nothing went to plan, but we didn't get caught.

We were fast to go back to Dad's car and drive straight out from the area before someone called the police. So far, no one has reported our SUV to the cops, so it appears we are in the clear.

I'm almost in two minds about the whole thing. On one hand, I'm glad we both made it through the night without either of us being arrested or worse, but on the other, I feel like we got away with something. No amount of jail time could ever punish me for what I did to Marie.

Dad asks me on a loop if I'm okay. He can see it in my eyes, a change within my core that is slowly resonating out to my entire persona.

"Can I get you anything from room service?" he asks me from his twin bed for a second time.

"No thank you." The thought of food makes me sick. Who could desire a single bite to eat after what we experienced? I stare at him as he flicks through the pages of the menu, trying to decide what the right choice is to make before he contacts the kitchen service. What if he orders the wrong thing? Will he ever forget it?

My heart beats so hard in my chest I have to force myself to get up out of my bed. "I'm going for a walk," I blurt.

"Okay. Don't stray too far. We'll be heading to the airport in about an hour or so."

I don't answer as I step by a bag full of all the items I packed up from Marie's house. As Beth, I kept my possessions to a bare minimum. I had to be prepared to be able to pack up and run at any time as if I never lived there. We had no rental agreement on paper, and we'd paid Marie my share of the rent in cash. There was nothing to trace back to us.

When I reach the elevator at the end of the hall, I press the button and see my reflection in the metal of the doors. I look like hell. Bloodshot eyes, frayed hair, and blotchy skin. I feel as if I've aged a decade in as little as a few days.

The elevator dings and opens in front of me. No one is inside to share the ride down fifteen floors which I'm not unhappy about. As I shuffle into the car, I turn to reach for the button for the lobby and see a small advertisement fixed to the wall above the array of floor choices. My hand freezes in the air before I can hit the circle as the ad grabs my attention.

An image of a perfect beach stares back at me with text describing the ultimate getaway to a tropical paradise. I think of Champagne Beach in Vanuatu. She dreamed of going there, believing she deserved to despite all the pain she caused. I stopped that from ever happening when I decided to let her die. Dad could have saved her. The rest of her injuries weren't so bad that she wouldn't have recovered from them.

My hand draws away from the lobby button.

A second later, I find myself back out in the hallway, headed for the stairs. I shove through the heavy door and feel the wobble in my legs collapse me down in seconds. Before I know it, I'm pressed into a concrete corner with my head against the wall, tears flowing.

Why did I let her die? Why did I allow my thirst for revenge take over at a time when I was in no state to make such a decision?

I'm not crying for her. I'll never shed a tear for that woman. She tried to kill Dad even when he was willing to meet her halfway. She deserved to pay for what she did to our family. Whether death was the correct punishment will be an internal debate that may rage on for the rest of my life. No, the reason I'm crying is far worse.

I once asked Marie what she was afraid of. At the time, I was trying to gauge how best to mess with her if Dad and I ever found out she was Tommy's killer. When Dustin told us everything only a few days later, I knew I would use the answer against her.

Dustin surprised me at the Denver hotel. He seemed like he was mad at us for daring to come to him in the first place, but something inside him burst like a dam when he spoke. Perhaps seeing the two of us after five long years still determined to find the truth got to him. Whatever the reason, he led us to the end.

Although Marie never told me with words, I could see it in her eyes the thing she feared more than anything else in the world: to die alone.

I held her hand when she died. But it wasn't to give her comfort in her last moments. It was my attempt to show her my contempt for the life she chose to live with the disappointed look I had on my face. I wanted her to understand that she destroyed my family and only showed remorse for the impact it had on her life. She always felt she had suffered from shooting Tommy, but no amount of self-absorbed pain would ever make up for her pointless actions.

Whether she acknowledged what I had attempted to show her in her dying seconds, I'll never know. All I can be certain of is I never want to be like Marie. I never want to feel above the choices I've made, the good and the bad. Does it mean I'll turn myself in for letting her bleed out in the street? Probably not. I can't leave Dad on his own to process these last few days. We need each other now more than ever.

The door to the stairwell opens. Dad pokes his head through and sees me crying in the corner like a kid who's done the wrong thing. "Toni. I thought I'd find you here."

I try to wipe my tears away in a hurry, but my eyes are red, and my nose is runny. There's no hiding what I'm doing.

Dad walks through and places his hands in his pockets as he leans against the wall beside me. "Do you mind if I join you?"

"No."

He settles in next to me and doesn't utter a word. We spend a few minutes in a comfortable silence that stops my tears from returning. The fact that he knew where to find me is enough to calm me down.

"Did I ever tell you about what motivated me to become an EMT?"

"No. I always figured you just wanted to help people."

"That's a good reason, but I'm afraid your old man isn't that selfless. It was to impress your mother."

"Really?" I look up to him.

"Yeah. We'd had you a few years earlier than we planned and were two clueless first-time parents trying to figure out the way things worked when you had a young baby in the house. You were about three months old when I lost my job at the plant in a wave of layoffs. It came at a terrible moment when we had hardly any savings in the bank to keep our heads above water."

I let a smile form on my face. Dad wasn't one to speak about the past like this. I had often tried to get him talking about the old days, but he never liked to reminisce.

"To make matters worse, you got sick with a vicious cold. It was the last thing we needed, but you can't tell life what it's allowed to throw at you. Anyway, we tried to get you better doing everything the doctor told us, but nothing seemed to work on that damn sickness of yours. You only got worse to the point where your mother freaked out and called an ambulance when your breathing became too shallow one night."

"No kidding."

"Yeah, you almost died on us, but the EMTs came and were amazing. I'll never forget the way they took control of the situation and made us feel so reassured everything would be okay. Your mother was beyond impressed by these people. You could see it in her eyes. As soon as we left the hospital, I looked into becoming an EMT."

I smiled up at him. It took a few years from what I'd heard, but Dad worked his butt off to complete his training and study.

"If you're wondering why I'm telling you this, it's because I think I need to go back to being an EMT. It's what your mother would have wanted. I know it. I just have to push myself."

"That's really awesome, Dad. I think it's a fantastic idea."

"It is, but I want you to know that I'm not going to push you back into school or work until you decide it's what you want, okay? You've been through enough recently."

I have been through a lot. I'd squeezed in too many painful up and downs into a short period. When we get home, I won't know what to do with myself. Not having what felt like an endless goal begging for my attention will be strange.

"Thanks, Dad." I feel some weight on my shoulders lifting away.

I thought the only way we were ever going to find peace was to force Marie to pay for what she did to Tommy. The more I think about it, the more I realized what we did in her home failed to ease the burden my and Dad's lives had become. Her confession didn't bring Tommy back as much as letting her die did. I can't help but question where we would be today if we had moved on and never given Marie another thought.

We both stare ahead at the grimy stairwell in silence. One flight leads up. The other down. Where we go from here is a choice only we can help each other make.

The End